"Stop grinning," Summer insisted.

Eben bit his lip to keep back the laughter as he handed Summer another napkin. He watched as she wiped most of the gooey egg off her shorts and leg. Summer Hudson's legs in rolled-up jeans were fantastic, but in shorts they were dynamite: smooth and tanned. "Come on, let's go into the kitchen to wash that off."

Summer glared at him. "Why, don't you like flies buzzing around you?"

He turned his laugh into a cough and pulled her into the house. After wetting a paper towel, he knelt in front of her.

Heat burned a path up her leg wherever the cool towel touched. She felt her heart start to pound and her breath come in hurried gasps. There it was again, the attraction she'd felt the other night. Only now it was growing hotter. His hand scorched her calf as he tenderly held her leg still. Her voice was low and jerky as she whispered, "I can do that."

Eben looked up and desire flooded his body when he saw her eyes darken. "It was my fault for throwing it too hard."

She was breathless. "I should have caught it."

The cool towel traveled over her knee. "No, you should have told me you had never been in an egg toss before." Eben's hand tightened on the back of her knee as he finished cleaning her leg. Not a trace of egg was left on the dewy skin. He felt the slight tremor of her leg and closed his eyes.

The countertop bit into her hand as Summer grabbed it for support. Not sure if she was calling him in need or pushing him away, she cried out his name. "Eben. . . ."

WHAT ARE *LOVESWEPT* ROMANCES?

They are stories of true romance and touching emotion. We believe those two very important ingredients are constants in our highly sensual and very believable stories in the *LOVESWEPT* line. Our goal is to give you, the reader, stories of consistently high quality that may sometimes make you laugh, sometimes make you cry, but are always fresh and creative and contain many delightful surprises within their pages.

Most romance fans read an enormous number of books. Those they truly love, they keep. Others may be traded with friends and soon forgotten. We hope that each *LOVESWEPT* romance will be a treasure—a "keeper." We will always try to publish

LOVE STORIES YOU'LL NEVER FORGET
BY AUTHORS YOU'LL ALWAYS REMEMBER

The Editors

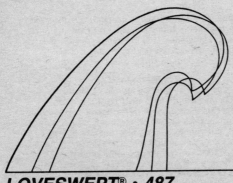

LOVESWEPT® • 487

Marcia Evanick
Sizzle

BANTAM BOOKS
NEW YORK • TORONTO • LONDON • SYDNEY • AUCKLAND

SIZZLE

A Bantam Book / August 1991

ISBN 0-553-44129-9

Published simultaneously in the United States and Canada

To my son, Michael—
created in love,
nourished with love.
May you always know the joy.

Love,
Mom

One

She didn't come tonight.

Eben James slowly rose from the canvas deck chair and scanned the beach behind his house one last time. For the past three evenings, just after work, he had sat on the deck and watched a lone figure stroll down the beach and back. The first time he saw her, she was walking, shin deep, in the water and paying close attention to the surface of the lake. She didn't even glance toward his house. The second night she had stopped, spotted him, and raised a hand in greeting. He had returned the greeting, and last night's too. But tonight she didn't come.

Eben walked to the wooden railing, then turned to face the house. The entire back wall consisted of glass sliding doors that framed the lake. Three years ago he had argued with the architect about the amount of fuel it would take to heat the house. The architect had pointed out that it was sacrilegious to live by the lake and not show it. Eben had finally agreed to the design and came to appreciate the breathtaking view, even when his electric bill soared in the dead of winter. The peaceful serenity of the lake had become his companion.

So why wasn't he feeling calm after viewing his serene companion for the past hour? With a frown he entered the kitchen and proceeded to heat a frozen dinner in the microwave. As the gentle electric hum filled the kitchen, Eben walked back to the sliding doors and stared out at the shore. Why hadn't she come?

"Damn, this is ridiculous!" he exclaimed with exasperation. Then he realized he was talking to himself. *A sure sign you are losing it, old boy. And all because of a nameless woman who strolls down the beach.* Maybe it had been a little too long since his last relationship. When he had come home from work he had hurriedly dressed in a pair of jeans, sneakers, and a pullover top, intending to go down and introduce himself and finally put a name to the vision who had haunted his dreams the night before. Only she didn't show up.

The beep of the microwave interrupted his musing. With a scowl he placed the hot tray on the table and poured himself a glass of milk. He pushed the "generous serving" of wrinkled peas around and grimaced when he bit into a piece of meat that wasn't heated all the way through. Why did he bother with frozen dinners? He knew how to cook, but cooking for one was more of a hassle than it was worth. He got up from the table, dumped his remaining dinner in the trash, and placed his fork and glass into the dishwasher, which held a coffee cup and a plate from breakfast.

Eben slammed the dishwasher closed, knowing he

was acting childish. Self-pity was a childish emotion, and he deplored childish emotions. He grabbed his windbreaker from the hall closet and headed out to the deck. What he needed was a walk along the shore to burn off some of his excess energy.

Halfway down the wooden stairs that led to the shore of Lake Champlain, his feet faltered. She was coming! The nameless beachcomber was slowly making her way along the beach and pulling something that was large and orange.

Summer Hudson tugged on the wagon handle and lightly cursed the rocks and pebbles that were slowing her progress. If this rate continued, she'd never make it to the cove in time. The front wheel of the wagon struck a large rock, jostling her precariously balanced cargo. A sound of distress escaped her lips as she quickly grabbed the orange raft to keep it from toppling over. She gave a start when a deep voice sounded behind her.

"It works better when it's in water."

Summer quickly turned around and gazed up into a pair of smiling deep brown eyes. So his eyes were brown! For the past three evenings she had noticed him sitting on the deck of the most gorgeous house she had ever seen. She had a bet going with herself as to what color his eyes were. She had won. And pizza for dinner tomorrow night was her prize.

She scanned his tan features and realized he was more handsome than she had imagined. Viewing him from a distance of twenty-five yards didn't do him justice. Neatly cut and freshly combed brown hair made her fingers itch with the desire to run through it. His jaw was lightly shadowed, giving his white teeth more brilliance. Nicely shaped lips, straight and narrow nose, and well-defined cheekbones completed the nearly perfect picture.

Summer's heart lurched when her gaze met his equally scrutinizing stare. Saints preserve her, the man actually caused goose bumps to pop out in some of the most unusual places on her body. One saying from her childhood flashed through her mind: First impressions are so important. If this was his initial impact, she'd better double her insurance. He might prove to be fatal. She shifted her weight and forced a smile to her mouth. She hoped she looked at ease, calm, and in control.

Eben didn't miss a single expression that crossed her delicate face. He had not meant to startle her, but now he was glad he had. It had given him a chance to catch her unaware before the pleasant expression masked the interesting gleam that had shone in her eyes. Wanting to throw her off balance again, he stuck out his hand and smiled. "Eben James, and you are trespassing."

Summer's hand stopped an inch away from his and she frowned, wondering what was going on. She saw the laughter in his eyes and tentatively took his hand. "I'm sorry."

Eben sadly shook his head. "Did anyone ever tell you that your mother misnamed you? You don't look like a Sorry."

The warmth of his hand penetrated her palm as she chuckled. Even the saints would not be able to help her now. The man possessed a sense of humor. "The name is Summer Hudson, and I'm *sorry* for trespassing."

He gazed at her golden curls and sparkling blue eyes. The name Summer suited her, for she looked like sunshine. Her flawless face was lightly tanned, except for her nose and cheekbones, which were pink from sunburn. Summer was living up to her name. Fascinated by her windswept appearance, he said, "You have to pay the penalty, you know."

Summer glanced away from the charming stranger to the lowering sun. There was no way she was going to make it on time with the wagon. She should have started an hour earlier. Maybe she should scrap the idea for the night and focus her attention on Eben James. She needed to find out whether he was interested in her or was simply an extremely friendly person. "What's the penalty?" she asked curiously.

Eben was bewitched by her soft voice. Tight jeans, scruffy sneakers, and a baggy turquoise T-shirt gave her the appearance of a waif. Who was she, where did she come from, and where was she going?

He quickly glanced at her left hand—no rings there—and then at the huge inflatable raft. Opportunity only knocks once, and it was rapping on his door in the form of a raft. Who was he to argue? "I have to escort you to wherever you are hauling Jacques Cousteau's *Calypso II.*"

Excitement raced through Summer. He wanted to help. "If we hurry, I can still make it."

He blinked as Summer thrust the raft into his arms. As though mystified, he stood, transfixed, while she hauled the rusty wagon up to his steps and proceeded to unload it. She hung a camera and a pair of expensive binoculars around her neck, then grabbed two black plastic oars, an overstuffed tote bag, and a thermos.

Summer had taken a few steps along the shore when she realized Eben still wasn't moving. "Please hurry." She glanced at her watch. "It's almost time."

"Almost time for what?" Eben asked, but she didn't hear. She had already started down the beach once more. He frowned at the raft. What was she up to? More importantly, what was he doing? With a shrug, he maneuvered the bulky raft into its only possible carrying position, on top of his head. With a curse, he started to follow the enticing view of a denim-clad backside gently swaying down the beach.

Summer turned her head to check on Eben and had to bite the inside of her cheek to keep from giggling at the picture he made. It really was sweet of him to help. When they reached the cove, maybe she'd try asking personal questions, like "are you married, engaged, or criminally insane?" There had to be a reason why someone as gorgeous as Eben was still single.

She sighed as she bent under the low overhanging branches of a gigantic white pine. It was a shame to take the raft out on the lake that night; getting to know Eben might prove more fascinating.

Eben gulped a lungful of air when he spotted Summer coming to a halt at the lake's edge. Finally! This wasn't exactly what he had planned when he'd introduced himself. He'd pictured a quiet stroll along the shore and a friendly conversation. For the past half mile the only thing he had communicated with was an annoying mosquito that buzzed around his face, and the words he'd muttered weren't fit for a lady to hear. Summer had marched a frustrating thirty feet in front of him and occasionally looked over her shoulder to flash a dazzling smile and to inquire how he was doing. She acted like Stanley or Livingstone exploring the great continent while tramping over the seldom-used path, skirting pine trees, and generally being cheerful.

When Summer had bypassed the shoreline and headed into the pines, he knew he had gotten more than he had bargained for. All he wanted was to meet the enchanting beachcomber, not get a hernia. The raft was not heavy, just awkward to maneuver around, under, and through the huge pines and overgrown bushes that crowded the rarely used trail. He glanced around the isolated cove. He'd never been here before, though he'd passed it many times while he was out in his boat. The desire to hike through dense underbrush to explore it never materialized in him. A dozen colorful ducks were swimming close to shore, while others were waddling over the stone-splattered shoreline. "Now what?"

Summer jerked around, held her finger against her lips, and shushed him. She watched as a group of mallards quickly swam to the other side of the cove. Without a sound she raised the binoculars and scanned the smooth surface of the cove and lake. Satisfied, she lowered them and moved closer to Eben. "Thank you again for carrying the raft," she whispered.

Her gaze ran over his broad shoulders and trim waist. Lord, he was the best-looking pack mule she'd ever seen. She placed the oars, tote bag, and thermos into the raft. Keeping her voice low, she said, "I made it in plenty of time, thanks to you." She kicked off her sneakers and rolled up the bottom of her jeans. "I'm told twilight is the best time."

"Time for . . ." Eben frowned. "You're not going out alone in that raft, are you?"

Summer straightened to her full height of five feet five. "Of course I am," she answered. "What did you think I was going to do?"

Eben's frown turned into a full-blown scowl. "You can't go out in the raft alone."

Summer's golden eyebrows arched, and her chin tilted up. "Says who?"

"Common sense should tell you that you don't go out on a lake alone, especially without a life preserver." Eben walked over to a huge boulder and sat down. His movements were smooth and precise as he untied his shoelaces and took off his sneakers.

"But I do have . . ." She was too shocked to finish her protest. He was taking off his socks, rolling them into neat little balls, and placing them inside the gleaming white sneakers. Eben James was a perfectionist! No, the Fates wouldn't be so cruel as to have her living next door to a perfectionist for the next six weeks. She concentrated on the way he was rolling up his jeans. Without a ruler it was hard to tell, but she was sure there wasn't a quarter of an inch difference in the cuffs.

"Get in the raft, Summer. I'll push us off."

She glanced down at his feet and smiled. Eben couldn't be a perfectionist. He had the longest, skinniest, and ugliest toes she had ever seen. If he was one of those dreaded perfectionists who roamed the world, he would have gotten plastic surgery to correct this obvious imperfection.

Eben shifted his weight and wished she would stop staring at his toes. He had been self-conscious of his toes ever since an old girlfriend claimed they were the ugliest things she'd ever seen and jokingly requested that from then on he wear socks to bed. Summer didn't look repulsed. Instead she was looking at his bare feet with an endearing smile.

He was coming with her! She'd be alone in a raft for the next couple of hours watching the sunset with Eben. Maybe tonight was touched with magic and anything was possible. She waded through a couple of inches of water and climbed into the raft. "Nice and easy. Try not to make any more noise than absolutely necessary."

Eben glanced at the ducks. They seemed to be ignoring the fact that people were around and didn't seem agitated or upset. So why was Summer so nervous? He gently pushed the raft out another foot and carefully clambered aboard.

Summer picked up an oar and handed the other one to Eben. With smooth, sure strokes they paddled silently out to the middle of the cove. She smiled her thanks as she gave Eben the stuffed tote bag to hold. The dripping paddles and their feet were causing a small puddle to form in the bottom of the raft, and she didn't want it to become soaked. She shifted around on the slightly raised seat and brought the binoculars up to her eyes. She slowly scanned the lake's surface as the sun started its descent, tinting the shimmering water pink.

Nothing. No boats, lumps, or bumps broke the surface.

Eben's brows came together in concentration. What was she looking for? He turned his head and studied the floating party of ducks. Why wasn't she looking at them? Weren't they the reason for all this?

He watched, bemused, as she checked her camera and continued to glance at the empty lake.

Summer examined the lowering sun and checked her watch. This was the right time and place. Now all she needed was luck.

"What are you looking for?" Eben whispered.

She glanced at him and wondered if he was going to be her good luck charm. Her face held anticipation and excitement when she leaned closer to him and whispered, "Champ."

Eben's mouth fell open. He couldn't have been more surprised if she had stood up and started talking in tongues. He had to have misunderstood what she had said. "What did you say?"

"Champ." At his blank look she explained. "Surely you have heard of the legendary sea monster of Lake Champlain."

Eben slowly nodded his head without taking his eyes off her.

"He was seen in this area twice in the past five years. That's why I picked this spot." She was just warming up to her favorite subject. Still keeping her voice low, she continued. "Most of his sightings happen at twilight. That's when the night claims the day, or the day claims the night. This is the perfect opportunity to spot him, and I owe it all to you."

"Me!" Eben roared.

"Shhh. Keep your voice down." She glanced over at the ducks flapping their wings in agitation and frowned. "Do you want to scare off Champ?" Her scowl smoothed out as the ducks settled down. "You're the one who helped me carry the raft. If it wasn't for you, I would have had to postpone this watch."

Astonished, he asked, "Are you a scientist?"

Summer chuckled. "No, I'm an elementary school teacher."

"Then you ought to know there are no such things as sea monsters," Eben snapped. He was frustrated over being hoodwinked by a beautiful blonde into watching for a sea monster. What was the world coming to if a grown man couldn't even take a quiet walk along the beach without running into a loony?

Distressed by his words, she studied his expression. Asylum commitment for her was written all over his face. She raised the binoculars and quickly turned away before he could notice the moisture gathering in her eyes. The magic had died.

Eben had seen her hurt look and muttered a curse. He hadn't meant to hurt her, but hell, what did she expect? No sane woman would willingly admit she believed in sea monsters. Still he had to suppress a chuckle. No sane man would be stuck out in the middle of the lake looking for one either. There was a lesson buried in there somewhere, but he couldn't place his finger on it.

He gazed at her profile as she continued to scrutinize every ripple on the lake. She didn't look like a person who spent all her spare time stacking marbles in a corner. He swallowed hard as a light breeze molded the turquoise T-shirt to her chest. It had definitely been too long since his last relationship, he decided. His gaze run down her tight jeans and lingered on her well-shaped calves. Her dainty feet tapered into exquisite toes, each topped with peach-colored nail polish. Warmth spread through his abdomen as he imagined what her legs looked like. He'd bet anything they were tanned and smooth to the touch.

Eben shifted into a more comfortable position and pulled his mind away from Summer's legs. Why should it matter to him how her legs would feel? She was not his type! His brain had already received that message, now if only his body would cooperate.

He balanced the bulky tote bag on his lap and forced himself to watch the sun set over the distant Adirondacks. When was the last time he had watched a sunset? The splendor of the sunrise woke him nearly every morning as light came streaming in through his bedroom windows overlooking the lake. But his house was surrounded on three sides by huge, massive pines that blocked the sunset. Maybe he ought to thank Summer for giving him the opportunity to appreciate the beauty of this daily miracle.

Summer got herself under control and wondered what to do with Eben now. Throwing him overboard came to mind, but she quickly squashed that idea. It wasn't his fault he didn't possess an imagination. Finding a perfectionist with an imagination was as impossible as spotting a brontosaurus in downtown Chicago. The kind just didn't exist. However, it was amazing that Eben possessed a sense of humor; that in itself was extraordinary.

She should have listened to her common sense when he'd neatly rolled up his socks. "Perfectionist" had screamed from his every move then. But his toes had thrown her off balance, allowing him to slip under her guard. She lowered the binoculars, and under the guise of reaching for a sweatshirt that was buried in the tote bag, she glanced at the offending extremities.

They weren't as bad as she'd originally thought. Granted, they were long and thin but "ugly" was too harsh a word to describe them. "Interesting" captured them better. If Eben played footsies it could get mighty interesting.

She handed Eben her camera and binoculars, then pulled on her old University of Minnesota sweatshirt. As she shook her hair and slipped the equipment back over her head, she said, "Thanks."

Eben watched the last rays of the evening sun tint her golden hair a warm apricot color. How could a woman look so beautiful with apricot-colored hair? "You're welcome."

Summer fidgeted with the camera strap. She didn't need this problem on her vacation. Eben was sending out mixed signals. On one hand he seemed to feel the same physical attraction she was experiencing. But on the other he flat out denied the existence of Champ, without hearing one iota of evidence. The smartest thing she could do was head the raft to shore, deposit Mr. Skeptic, and get on with her life. "Do you want to go back?"

Of course he wanted to. What normal man would want to spend an evening with a loony who couldn't tell the difference between reality and fantasy? So why did he look into her earnest blue eyes and mutter, "No, I'll stay?" Bemused, he turned his attention back to the sunset and the gang of squawking ducks.

Summer adjusted the binoculars and concentrated on a widening ripple. Great, now she was stuck in a rubber dinghy with a gorgeous man and she couldn't think of a thing to say to him. "Have you lived here long?"

"About three years. I was born and raised in Albany." He moved his feet out of the cold puddle. He knew she wasn't a native of Pine Harbor. There was no way he could live there and not have noticed her. "Did you just move here?"

"No, I'm renting a cabin from the Beamsters."

The sun disappeared, casting the water into grayness. It figured, she was staying next door to him. "How long are you staying?"

"Till the middle of August," she answered, studying the lake. This was it. Twilight was upon them.

Eben sat up a little straighter. It was eery the way the ducks suddenly became silent. Even the breeze died. Nothing stirred. He pulled up the collar of his jacked and scowled. This was ridiculous. There are no such things as sea serpents, he told himself. So why, at this moment, was he feeling anything was possible?

Summer raised her camera and looked through the viewer at the darkening waters. She heard an owl hoot in the distance and suppressed a chuckle when Eben jerked. He was feeling it too. The air was heavy with power, and the peaceful lake was turning sinister. Anything was possible.

In total silence they sat as the last glimmer of daylight faded.

Summer lowered her camera and sighed. "Nothing." She replaced the lens cap and glanced at the barely visible shore. "Do you want a cup of coffee before we head back?"

Eben restrained his irrational desire to comfort her. "Did you pack enough for two?"

"I always bring extra provisions. You never know what you might encounter." She reached for the thermos. "Somewhere in the tote there's an extra cup. You don't mind cream and sugar, do you?"

"I usually take it black, but right now anything hot would taste great." He pulled out a flashlight from the bag and turned it on. Shining it into the tote, he tugged out a compact orange life preserver. "You did have one."

She shrugged. "I don't leave the shore without it."

"Why didn't you put it on tonight?"

No use bringing up the fact that she wanted to get to know him better, she decided. "I figured you could save me if I fell overboard."

Eben laid the preserver down and rummaged through the bag's contents. He pushed aside a box of chocolate chip cookies, a first-aid kit, and two flares before he located a plastic mug. He jammed the preserver back in and held out the cup.

Summer poured the coffee. "There are cookies in there if you're hungry."

"No thanks, this is fine." Eben blew on the hot liquid and tentatively sipped it. He had tasted better, and could imagine tasting worse, but it would do for now.

Summer quickly finished her coffee. Time to go. There was something too intimate about sitting in the dark with Eben and sharing a cup of coffee. She grabbed a paddle and started for the shore.

Eben followed suit, and in no time at all, they reached the cove. She rolled down her jeans and rubbed her damp feet with her sweatshirt before slipping on her sneakers. "I'll hold the flashlight for you," she said, taking it from him.

Eben sat down on the boulder he had used before. He unrolled a sock, used it to dry his foot, then put on a sneaker. The same treatment was given to his other foot. Placing the damp socks into his windbreaker pocket, he said, "Thanks. If you lead the way with the light, I'll be able to follow with the raft."

"The raft's not going back yet."

"It's not?"

"No. I'm going to need it before daybreak tomorrow morning, and it would be senseless to carry it back and forth." She shone the flashlight around, searching through the nearby bushes and trees. When she apparently found what she was looking for, she carried the raft, oars, and life preserver to a pine tree and concealed them under its low-hanging branches. "I don't think anyone comes here. These should be safe."

Eben frowned. He didn't like the idea of leaving the raft behind; it was obviously valuable. And the knowledge that she was coming back before daybreak alone sent a chill up his spine. Why should he be worried? She wasn't his responsibility. Still, he heard himself saying, "Be sure to wear the life preserver when you go out."

Summer glanced up at him. Was that concern she heard in his voice? "Always do when I'm alone." She picked up the tote and flashlight. "Do you want to lead, or would you rather I did?"

He took the tote and the flashlight from her. The evening hadn't turned out at all as he'd planned. His fantasy beachcomber was in reality a beautiful and independent nut who thought he was lost in the dark. "I think I can find my way back home," Eben snapped.

Summer flinched. "I didn't mean it the way you're taking it, Eben."

He swung the light to her face and saw her regretful expression. "I know you didn't, Summer." He ran a hand over his unshaven jaw. "It was just that I envisioned something different when I met you."

"Ah, now I get it. You were looking for an easy lay."

Two

Eben groaned. How could things have deteriorated so rapidly? Her elevator might not stop at all the floors, but she called the shots as she saw them. He was honest enough with himself to realize he had sought her out because he was physically attracted to her, but her accusation was completely untrue. "That's an interesting theory, but I had pictured a quiet dinner."

A heated flush of embarrassment flooded her cheeks. How could she have totally misjudged a person? "Dinner?"

He jerked the flashlight back to her face when he heard the apologetic tone of her voice. Warnings flashed in his mind. Summer Hudson was one dangerous woman. In an instant she had turned his logical thinking around. They were completely incompatible. What would they discuss over dinner— mermaids and little green Martians? "Look, Summer, you're a very beautiful woman, and yes, I do find you physically attractive, but I believe we're looking for different things in life. I'm going to have to pass on dinner."

Summer squinted into the light. So who asked you, she thought angrily.

"I wish you success on your . . . quest here in New York."

"Thank you." She forced a friendly smile on her lips. "It's getting awfully late. Don't you think we should head back?"

Eben opened his mouth, started to say something, then clamped it shut. She could have at least argued the point, he thought irrationally. He turned and headed down the path.

Summer followed at an even pace, trying hard not to stomp through the woods. Eben James was a dictatorial snob. Who did he think he was, suggesting dinner and then taking it back? She wouldn't have gone anyway—dinner with Eben would probably be as fun and exciting as hanging out the laundry—but that wasn't the point. She ducked under a low-hanging branch Eben was holding back for her. "Thanks," she muttered.

They probably would have spent the entire date talking about his job. Though she wondered what he did for a living, there was no way she was going to ask. The fewer things she knew about him, the better off she'd be. His occupation was guaranteed to be boring, she bet. He was a desk jockey if she ever saw one.

She glanced at his nicely shaped backside and felt a blush sweep up her cheeks. She hadn't really said that about him taking her to bed, had she? Lord, what had come over her? The Summer Hudson she knew back in Iowa would never have uttered those words. Maybe it was the altitude. Her eyes traveled back to worn denim clinging to lean hips. Maybe it was the company?

They emerged from the dense pine forest and headed silently down the beach. The lights on Eben's deck could be seen glowing in the distance. Even his house was perfect. Summer turned away from the welcoming sight and gazed out across the lake. Had she remembered to turn her porch light on?

When they reached his house, Eben lowered the tote bag into the rusty wagon. "I'll walk you home."

Summer shook her head. "Thanks, but you've already done enough." She took the flashlight and grabbed the handle of the wagon.

"It'll be hard pulling the wagon by yourself."

"I managed to get it here, I can manage to get it back." She started to walk away. "Good night, Eben."

Eben watched as she yanked the wagon over rocks. "Summer?"

"Yeah?"

"Thanks for the coffee."

Summer's foot stumbled for a moment. "Sure, anytime."

Eben sat on the bottom steps as the lone figure slowly made her way down the shore. When she disappeared into the trees, he released a long sigh.

Moonlight shimmered and bounced across the lake. He didn't find any comfort in the water tonight. Instead his silent, serene companion for the past three years seemed to be having a good laugh at his expense.

• • •

Summer set the alarm clock for an ungodly hour, turned off the light, and climbed in between yellow sheets. An owl hooted in the distance, and she wondered if it could be the same owl they had heard earlier. Even Eben had felt the uncontrolled energy that surrounded them during those few precious moments of twilight. She hadn't been able to tell if the power came from the air, lake, or themselves.

She rolled over onto her side and buried her face in the pillow. Who cared what Eben thought? Imagine getting physical proof of Champ's existence! Someone had to be the first one to take his picture, and it might as well be her.

Lists of places she had to check out and people to talk to filtered through her sleepy brain, effectively pushing Eben James to the dark recesses of her mind.

Eben stood in his boxer shorts and watched Summer hurrying down the beach. She was running late. Daylight would be breaking soon. The beam of her flashlight bounced across rocks and skimmed the surrounding area. Within moments she was lost from sight.

He muttered a curse and headed back to his now-cool bed. He had been looking out the huge panes of glass for the past half hour. He climbed in between the sheets and frowned. Why had he awakened? When he had gone to bed the previous night, he had firmly put his intriguing, eccentric neighbor out of his thoughts. He had concentrated on a new tax law and wondered which clients it was going to help and which ones it was going to hurt.

He fluffed his pillow and straightened out the blanket, trying to find a more comfortable position. Was she all right? Maybe he should have gone with her, he thought. How was she going to hold the flashlight and paddle at the same time? He reminded himself that it wasn't any of his business. He should stay out of her life. Still, he couldn't help wondering if she would remember to wear her life preserver. What if a boat plowed into her? How in the hell would a hunk of Styrofoam rescue her from a speeding boat?

Eben groaned and pressed a pillow over his head, hoping it would stop the asinine questions from running through his head. Summer was a mature woman who could obviously take care of herself.

What if she paddled too far and ended up stranded in the middle of the lake? She had flares with her; she could set one off.

What if the flare was faulty and set the raft on fire? She had plenty of water to put it out.

What if Champ rose his ugly head from the murky depths of Lake Champlain and gobbled her up?

With a cry of irritation and worry, Eben flung a navy blue pillow across the room. Then, muttering every dirty word he had ever read on men's room walls, he got up and yanked on a clean pair of jeans and a sweatshirt. He went out, locking the glass door behind him, and hurried down the steps, all the while chastising himself for being ridiculous and acting crazy. He was a sane man about to make a fool of himself.

• • •

Summer took another sip of coffee and glanced around. The lake was bathed in pale morning light and the sun was climbing over the Green Mountains of Vermont. Twilight had passed.

Two boats were in the distance, a boisterous group of ducks were swimming in circles by the shore looking for breakfast, and the silent forest was slowly awakening to a new day. Not another soul was in sight. So why did she have the feeling someone was watching her?

She replaced the cap on the thermos and paddled toward shore. She yanked the raft up on the beach, slipped out of the life preserver, and slid her feet into her sneakers. No one was around. She told herself she was imagining things as she hid the raft.

Summer rubbed the back of her neck and picked up the tote bag. It was lack of sleep that was causing her to feel jittery. By the time she had finally drifted to sleep the night before it was late, and the alarm had sounded only a few hours later. Maybe she should go back to her cabin and catch up on sleep. Going around all day feeling paranoid wasn't her idea of having fun on a vacation.

Eben slammed a folder closed and tossed his glasses on top of it. He rubbed the bridge of his nose and leaned back in the leather chair. His plan wasn't working. He had purposely stayed late at the office so he wouldn't be tempted to follow Summer again. That morning was bad enough.

While he had hidden in the woods and watched

her, like a Peeping Tom, he had realized Summer didn't need to be protected. She had shown concern for her own safety. A fluorescent orange preserver had been wrapped securely around her chest. He'd already known the tote bag carried a first-aid kit, flares, and enough supplies to last her a week on a deserted island. Since there were no uncharted islands in Lake Champlain, he would have to say she was overcautious.

Summer Hudson was also beautiful, and being a schoolteacher, obviously intelligent. She had a sense of humor and showed signs of being practical. She possessed every quality he was looking for in a woman, including an extra one thrown in for good measure—insanity.

Eben stood up, closed the blinds, and shut off the lights. Time to go home to a house that had suddenly developed too many rooms for one man.

Summer studied the twenty-eight dominoes lying facedown on the table in front of her. "Did you want me to pick all three at once?" she asked.

Aurora Dove smiled at the younger woman sitting across from her. "But of course."

Summer concentrated on the wooden rectangles and slowly moved three of them toward the woman who was her landlady for the next six weeks. She shifted uncomfortably in the kitchen chair as Aurora Dove glanced from the dominoes to her, and back again.

Summer hated to have her fortune told, but when Aurora Dove suggested reading it with dominoes, she was intrigued. She had never seen anyone interpret dominoes before, and anything that didn't have a Death card was fine with her. Once when she was twenty she had had her future told in a red-and-white-striped tent by a gypsy of undeterminable origin. She was nervous then too, only to be disappointed by the standard crystal-ball reading. *Traveling holds great importance in your future. You will meet a tall, dark stranger, fall in love, and be married.* In the six years since the prediction, she had met many tall, dark-haired strangers, but love never grew. Once she thought she had found the elusive emotion, only to be proven wrong.

Why had she allowed Aurora Dove to persuade her to sit through this again? Because she didn't want to hurt the woman's feelings, if truth be told. Summer's lips curved into a gentle smile as she watched Aurora Dove turn over the first domino. A black dot over a black dot. The sound of Franklin Beamster, Aurora Dove's husband, talking to someone in the living room registered in Summer's mind as she continued to look at the innocent tile. When Aurora Dove didn't speak, Summer wondered if she had turned over the domino of Death.

Aurora Dove tenderly caressed the two dots. "A stranger."

Summer bit back a groan. Great, another stranger in her future. Considering she was over a thousand miles from home, it didn't strike her as divine prophecy.

Aurora Dove turned over the next tile, four dots over three. "You are expecting disappointments?"

Summer glanced guiltily at the woman who had become her friend in the past four days. "Disappointments?"

"You won't be disappointed, Summer. You will find success and happiness."

Summer grinned. After years of searching, she was about to realize her dream. She, Summer Hudson, was going to prove to her parents that the unexplainable did exist. The smile stayed on her lips as Aurora Dove turned over the third and final domino. A double six lay faceup in the middle of the kitchen table.

Franklin whistled and when Summer turned around to look at him, she saw him pushing away from the wall where Eben was leaning.

Summer quickly glanced from Eben's scowl to Aurora Dove's amazed expression. Summer hadn't seen him for three days, and now he was here. "Is it good?"

Walking toward the table, Franklin whistled again. "The best, Summer, the best."

She looked at Aurora Dove and asked, "The best of what?"

Aurora Dove cradled the tile in the palm of her hand. "The best of everything, from happiness, success, money, and every other aspect of your life." She handed the domino to Summer. "I have never read such a promising future. Cherish it."

Summer studied the double-six tile. With reverence, she whispered, "I will." This domino wasn't referring to Champ; it was predicting the rest of her life. Did she dare believe it?

"Eben, I didn't even see you standing there," Aurora Dove said happily. "Summer, I would like to introduce you to our neighbor, Eben James. Eben, this is one of our guests, Summer Hudson. She is staying in cabin number six."

Eben moved away from the wall and sat on a chair. "Summer and I have already met." So this was where she was. When the sky had turned threatening and rain began to fall earlier that day he had started to worry. For the past few days he had forced himself to stay away from the cove, but as the distant sound of thunder grew nearer, he had grabbed his wind-breaker and flashlight and headed to the cove. He had breathed a silent prayer when he spotted the raft still concealed under the low-hanging pine branches. "Glad to see you have sense enough to come in out of the rain," he told Summer.

Summer's light blue eyes darkened as Eben's deep, smooth voice filled the room. She glanced at his wet jeans and damp hair. "It looks like one of us uses the common sense the good Lord gave us. Do you take moonlit strolls through thundershowers often?"

Eben wasn't sure who was more shocked, he or the Beamsters. Franklin went into a coughing fit, while Aurora Dove nearly choked with laughter. Here he had been tramping through rain-soaked woods to make sure she wasn't in trouble, and this was the thanks he received. He opened his mouth to tell her why he was out in the rain, but quickly closed it. How would he explain it without appearing interested? She'd split her side laughing if she knew how he had pounded on her cabin door. When he had spotted her car parked at the cabin, he figured she had to be around someplace, so he came running to Franklin to see if he had seen her.

Confused by the Beamsters' reactions, Summer asked, "Did I say something funny?"

Eben cleared his throat and glared at Aurora Dove until she quieted down. "It's just that I've never been accused of anything so . . ." He paused for a moment and searched for the correct word before saying "fanciful."

Summer watched as Eben accepted a beer from Franklin. He still seemed perfect, too perfect. The man had just spent the evening running around in a thunderstorm and he still looked immaculate. Even the stark white towel hanging around his neck gave him a rakish air. The yellow pullover brought out the hazel glints in his brown eyes, and she'd bet the gold watch gleaming on his wrist was telling the correct time. Her parents would love him.

She crossed her legs to hide the pizza stain on her jeans and willed the feeling of inadequacy to go away. Was it her fault that she had gotten too engrossed in Stephen King's bestseller to watch the time? She had planned on a quick shower before coming over to the Beamsters, but when she looked up at the clock, she was already ten minutes late. Aurora Dove and Franklin didn't seem to mind her lack of makeup or wrinkled blouse. At least the blouse was clean.

When Eben tilted the can up toward his mouth, she asked, "Don't you ever do anything fanciful?"

Eben choked on the mouthful of beer. Visions of the fanciful dream he had had the previous night flashed across his mind. It wasn't just fanciful, it was exotic.

Summer couldn't tell whether Eben's flush was caused by choking or private thoughts.

"Eben bought a high-powered little beauty of a boat that was designed for waterskiing," Franklin said. "He only uses it for fishing."

Aurora Dove placed two delicate teacups on the table and filled them with an aromatic brew. "You're

wrong, dear, it was the time he grew a mustache."
She pushed a cup in front of Summer. "Drink it while
it's hot. It's pennyroyal tea, and it will let you dream
in color."

Summer stared at the delicate porcelain cup with
its steaming brew. "It will?"

"Of course." Aurora Dove sipped from her cup. "It
isn't Eben's fault he's dull. The IRS won't let him do
anything creative."

Summer looked in awe at Eben. She had never met
anyone from the IRS before, and secretly prayed she
never would again. "You work for the IRS?" He was
probably the head honcho. She hadn't mentioned
anything illegal or sneaky the other day, had she?

"No, I'm a certified public accountant. Aurora Dove
is a little miffed at me still, because I wouldn't allow
her to claim the cost of her hypnotist on their income
tax."

"Hypnotist?"

"Not only does Aurora Dove dream in color, she has
several past lives too," Eben said with a chuckle.

Franklin winked and smiled reassuringly at Summer, while Aurora Dove lowered her teacup. "Eben, I
do believe you're jealous."

Incredulous, he asked, "Of what?"

"The fun I had in my past lives!"

"Fun! Didn't you tell me last month that in one of
your many lives you worked in a brothel in Texas?"

"How many women do you know who can say they
slept with Sam Houston?"

"Franklin, are you going to sit there and allow your
wife to talk like that?" Eben asked.

"Now, Eben, you and I both know that Aurora Dove
has a mind of her own. Besides, what she learned in

that brothel has become very dear to me in the past month."

Summer glanced over at Franklin's rough, weathered face and burst out laughing. The man belonged on the cover of an L. L. Bean catalog standing in front of a roaring fire with his hunting dogs at his feet, not sitting around a kitchen table discussing his wife's past lives. And he certainly didn't look like a man who would marry anyone named Aurora Dove.

Aurora Dove could have been anywhere between thirty-five and forty-five, with long golden hair that fell to her waist in a single braid. The traces of gray that were showing through the braid and a few minor wrinkles at the corners of her clear green eyes let the casual observer know she wasn't quite as young as she first appeared. Faded and ripped jeans, bare feet, and tie-dyed T-shirts were her usual outfit. Tonight she wore a green T-shirt with a huge peace sign across the chest. Her green eyes were starting to smolder as she gave her husband a heated look.

Eben groaned when he saw the intense look pass between husband and wife. "Ms. Hudson, I do believe it's about time we left."

Summer noted the look and agreed. "Thank you, Aurora Dove, for the reading and the cup of tea. I'll let you know tomorrow if I dreamt in color."

Franklin didn't take his eyes from his wife. "Eben, make sure you walk Summer home. It's dark outside, and we don't want her tripping over some root and breaking an ankle."

Eben stood up with Summer. "No problem, it's on my way." As they headed out of the kitchen, he called, "Remember the Alamo."

• • •

Summer thanked Eben as he opened her umbrella and held it high. The rain had tapered off to a light drizzle. She pulled on a pink raincoat with ducks wearing red galoshes printed all over it and stepped off the porch and under the umbrella. Eben shone a beam of light in front of her as they walked. "Do you and Aurora Dove always fight like that?"

"Only for the past three years."

"And before that?"

"I didn't know her then," Eben answered.

Summer smiled. The distant glow and sounds from the neighboring cabins filtered through the pine trees. The rutted road they were on was wide enough to drive a car on but treacherous in the dark. She carefully followed the trail lit by Eben. Curious, she asked, "Don't you believe in past lives either?"

"Sure, along with the man in the moon and the tooth fairy."

His answer didn't surprise her; it just confirmed what she had already guessed. Eben James, for all his good looks, hot vibrations, and sexy toes, was definitely not her type. She wasn't sure if she believed in past lives either, but she didn't dismiss the subject as easily as he did. Since all the facts weren't known on it, her mind was open.

Eben glanced at her and wondered what she was thinking. If she believed in sea monsters, she'd probably accept Aurora Dove's past lives. Wanting to know more about her, he asked, "Where do you live when you're not vacationing in New York?"

"I have an apartment in West Bend, Iowa."

"That explains the Midwest accent." He paused. "Do you share this apartment with anyone?"

Summer was tempted to tell him the entire Corn Huskers football team lived with her. He obviously thought she was a flake, so what difference could it make? "No, just me and a couple of plants."

He smiled and directed her around a large puddle. She appeared quite normal tonight; he was the one acting out of character. "What grade do you teach?"

"Second."

Her answer was polite enough, so why did he get the feeling she was holding back? Frustration caused by not understanding what made her tick made his voice rise. "Do you believe your future Aurora Dove read from *dominoes*?"

Summer halted in her tracks and tried to read his expression. "Let's say I would rather believe that my future holds great happiness and success than to believe it holds nothing."

Amused, he asked, "Won't you be disappointed if you don't achieve great happiness and success?"

"Yes, I will be. But at least I'll know I tried."

Eben heard the sarcasm, directed toward him, in her voice. A drop of cold water from his hair ran down the back of his shirt. His jeans were damp, and his new sneakers were squishing with every step. His heart was still pounding from when he couldn't find her in the storm, and he hadn't gotten a decent night's sleep since he met her. "Why do you persist in looking for a legend? Isn't anything in the real world good enough for you?"

Summer considered his question, and when she answered, her voice was low and thoughtful. "Maybe there's nothing in the real world worth looking for."

She brought her hand up to shield her eyes as Eben aimed the light in her face. "What's that supposed to mean?"

With a shrug she turned away and headed up the steps to her cabin. "I'm not sure, Eben. I'm not sure."

Eben followed her up to the small porch, closed the umbrella, and leaned it against an old rocker. He studied her in the faint light coming from one of the windows. Summer had forgotten to turn the porch light on. Why had she sounded so depressed? "I don't understand what you mean."

Summer gave a dry chuckle. "Perfect people don't have to understand, Eben. They either accept or condemn."

"Perfect people?"

Summer unlocked her door and turned the knob. "Perfect people still exist in this day and age. They're as uncommon as tornadoes in the desert, but they still ramble the world, causing devastation wherever they touch down."

"What's that got to do with me?"

"You're one of them, Eben. You see everything in black or white. There's no gray in your world."

Astonished, he gasped. "I'm perfect?"

Summer tightened her hold on the knob. Enduring awkward moments wasn't on her vacation list of things to do. She had spent enough time suffering through that in the past. "Listen, Eben, you were right the other night. We have absolutely nothing in common." She opened the door. "It was nice of you to help me out the other night, and I hope you find happiness in life."

Eben snapped his mouth shut and blinked. First, she called him perfect, then she wished him a happy life. Well, there was one thing he was going to do before he walked out of her life. He stepped in front of the door and did what he had been dreaming of doing since he first met her. He kissed her.

Summer saw his intent too late. As his mouth covered hers she stiffened in shock. When his kiss gently softened to a tender caress, she melted in his arms. Her arms encircled his neck as she returned the sweet, undemanding pressure.

Eben felt her body's surrender and groaned. What in the hell was he doing? He gently broke the kiss, before it had the chance to grow into something he wouldn't be able to control, and stepped back. He studied her dazed expression in the pale light, waiting for a slap across the face. Anything would be better than her silence. For the first time he had kissed a woman who obviously wasn't interested. But he had wanted to kiss her, so he did. What he owed her now was an apology. "That was . . ."

"Perfect too." Summer completed his sentence and lowered her arms. She stepped into the cabin and softly whispered, "Good-bye, Eben."

Eben watched the door shut and heard the clicking of the lock. She had said, "Good-bye," not "Good night," "See you around," or "Thanks for the lovely evening," but "Good-bye," as in "*Adios*, hit the road, Jack." Well, who could blame her? He'd grabbed her on the porch and kissed her speechless. Granted, she did participate, and she had called it perfect. So what was her problem? He knew she had a flaw. A flaw, hell, she was Don Quixote with a bra. She was out chasing sea serpents instead of windmills.

He looked at the closed door for over a minute before stepping off the porch and heading home. As he threaded his way through the pine trees and occasional raindrops, he realized they had more in common than they both had known. That kiss wasn't one-sided.

Summer glared at the painting mounted above the fireplace. She had done it again. She was attracted to another *perfect* man. Last year it had been a banker, now a CPA. What next? A Republican congressman from Des Moines? One thing was for certain—she was staying as far away from Eben James as humanly possible.

She walked over to the refrigerator and yanked on the stubborn door. Two empty bottles of soda, half a carton of milk, and three slices of pizza greeted her. She picked up a slice and promised herself she would go shopping tomorrow. Tonight she was tired and wanted to finish the Stephen King novel.

After reading the same page twice, Summer jammed a spoon between the pages and closed the book. Her entire concentration was thrown off by a kiss. It wasn't even a tongue-plunging, hand-roving, and hip-grinding kiss. It was a tentative and agreeable merging of two sets of lips that explored, tasted, and promised.

With a curse, Summer headed for the shower. This trait of being attracted to the wrong man had to be in her genes. All during high school she had dated nerds and twerps to keep her parents happy. In college, when her parents had poured on the pressure to find a suitable escort, she had rebelled and dated brawny, brainless jocks. By the time she graduated and started teaching, she had outgrown the need for rebelling against or pleasing her parents. Only problem was, she hadn't been interested enough in any man to form a relationship, until Richard.

Richard Lombard was the cream of the crop. He was the youngest executive ever to grace the offices of Iowa's Farmers Bank, and his career was just starting. Her parents adored him, the president of the bank considered him his prodigy, and parking spaces magically opened up for him. With his golden good looks, boyish charm, and smooth style, she had fallen in love within a week. By the end of the month they were engaged. But as her knowledge of Richard grew, the love she had for him withered and died. No one was more shocked than Richard when she broke the engagement the following month. Her parents were still fuming.

With a sigh she stepped out of the shower and toweled off. Richard was ancient history, over a year old. Maybe it was time for her to start thinking about another relationship. She wasn't getting any younger, after all. As she blow-dried her unruly curls she frowned. Eben James was definitely not relationship material, no matter how great his kisses were. Besides there were a thousand reasons why a relationship would have to wait until she returned home to Iowa; they were called miles. In six weeks she would be sweltering in her apartment preparing for the start of a new school year.

She turned off the lights and climbed in between the cotton sheets of the double bed. Summer willed the feeling of disappointment to go away. What more could she ask for in life? She was guaranteed happiness and success by Aurora Dove, and to top that, that night she was going to dream in color.

Three

Eben frowned as he glanced around at the crowded picnic tables and screaming kids. Why had he accepted Aurora Dove and Franklin's invitation to their annual Fourth of July barbecue? Every year they managed to pull together the strangest and loudest group of people since Woodstock.

He dodged a flying Frisbee and politely nodded to a group of men wearing black leather and chrome studs as he made his way over to Franklin, who was manning the grill. "Looks like you and Aurora Dove outdid yourselves this year."

Franklin smiled and flipped a row of sizzling hamburgers. "Glad you could make it, Eben."

Eben glanced around and frowned. "So, how many people are here?"

"Close to two hundred, counting the renters and out-of-towners."

Eben reached into a washtub filled with ice and

soda and pulled out a soft drink. "All your renters show up?"

"Why don't you just ask?" Franklin said with a chuckle.

"All right, is she here?"

With great care Franklin gave each of the thirty hot dogs a quarter turn. "Who?"

"Summer Hudson."

"Ah, you mean the cute little schoolteacher from cabin number six?"

Exasperated, Eben snapped, "Yes, her."

Franklin studied the grill he had made from cutting a fifty-five-gallon drum lengthwise, and started to turn the row of hamburgers again. "She's in the kitchen with Aurora Dove." Franklin looked at the house. "And Congressman Willis."

Eben frowned.

"Aurora Dove offered to teach Summer how to make Squash Surprise." He finished turning the last hamburger. "Never knew Willis was interested in cooking."

Eben gulped half the can of soda. He knew it would never work with Summer anyway; they would drive each other crazy. So why was his blood pressure rising at the thought of Willis panting after Summer? He smiled at the concerned look on Franklin's face. "You don't have to cook all day, do you?"

"No, Leonard is taking over at twelve."

A look of horror passed over Eben's face. "Please tell me he didn't bring his sister along!"

"Now, Eben, you know Leonard never goes anywhere without Mitzi," Franklin answered with mirth.

The day was ruined. If he left now, there was still time to join a group of friends who were celebrating up in South Hero. "Franklin, old pal, since your party is going great and is sure to top last year's, I think I'll be taking off."

"Gee, Eben, old pal," Franklin mimicked, "Mitzi has been asking about you for the past two hours. I told her you'd be here."

Eben opened his mouth to complain, when the back door of Franklin's house opened. Aurora Dove came bouncing out, laughing and carrying a huge bowl. Congressman Willis was smiling his wily smile, like a fox in the henhouse—or was that a fox in the congressional House?—and toting a larger bowl. Summer brought up the rear, bearing a dish covered in plastic wrap and forcing a smile to her lips.

Summer spotted Eben and stopped in her tracks. He came. She was half hoping he would and half dreading it. What was she going to say to him? In the two days since he had walked her home and kissed her, she had avoided walking past his house, but she couldn't stop thinking of him. Every instinct told her to run. So why were her feet cemented to the ground?

Eben had taken two steps toward Summer when a throaty voice of doom reached out and surrounded him. "Eben, darling, you're here!"

Summer's gaze shifted from Eben to the voluptuous woman who was throwing her arms around his neck. A red pouty kiss landed on his cheek as he tried to disengage her arms.

Eben looked back at Summer's expressionless face and groaned. What else could possibly go wrong? His question was answered as Willis came back and took the dish Summer was holding and gallantly escorted her to the tables overflowing with food. With a false smile Eben turned to the woman still plastered against him. "Well, hello, Mitzi, isn't this a surprise."

Summer carefully balanced the plate on her lap and took another sip of soda. Was she supposed to eat all this stuff? Aurora Dove had spotted her in line at the food table and insisted on filling the plate for her. Visions of a juicy hamburger vanished into thin air as Aurora Dove piled on the salad greens and nutty casseroles. With a silent groan she picked up her plastic fork and poked a weed. She knew rabbits who were eating better than this.

"Isn't the food great?" George Willis asked.

Summer painstakingly smiled. George Willis was the south end of a northbound skunk. The man was sitting there eating a hamburger with the works while she was supposed to munch on dandelion leaves. When she came to the party an hour before, he'd suddenly appeared next to her and hadn't budged since. The man didn't understand an I'm-not-interested-thank-you attitude even when it smacked him in the face.

George was store-bought handsome, Summer thought, noticing the colored contacts that made his eyes crystal blue. His teeth were capped, straightened, and polished to a dazzling glow, and his nose was too perfect not to have been fixed. He laughed at the appropriate times, asked the proper questions, and was evasive with every answer he gave. George Willis was going places in Washington, D.C. Only problem was, Summer wished he'd go places *now*, and leave her alone.

Before she could formulate an answer about the

food, Eben and the walking advertisement for silicone injections came over. "Mind if we join you?" Eben asked.

George looked up and nearly choked on a mouthful of potato salad. He muttered his permission and slid over without taking his eyes off Mitzi's abundant charms. She was dressed in red leather shorts and a tight navy blue tank top that glistened with white sparkling stars. Mitzi was more patriotic than Yankee Doodle.

Summer murmured an agreement and slid away from George. Why, when there were acres of places to sit, did Eben have to pick this spot? Wasn't it bad enough she had to put up with Gorgeous George and his creased pants? What kind of man wore two-tone loafers that matched his dark blue pants and light blue shirt? Real men weren't supposed to wear baby blue shoes on their feet.

"Mitzi, I would like to introduce you to Summer Hudson. She's renting a cabin for the next couple of weeks. And this is *Congressman* Willis." Eben purposely put the emphasis on "Congressman" and waited for Mitzi's reaction.

"A congressman!" Mitzi squealed.

Summer gritted her teeth.

Eben watched as Mitzi gleefully abandoned him and squirmed closer to Willis. "A real congressman?"

Summer pushed a chunk of squash from one side of her plate to the other while eyeing Eben's hamburger. She was trying not to drool.

Eben noticed the mound of uneaten grass clippings on Summer's plate and sighed. While Mitzi bubbled and Willis puffed out his chest, he took Summer's plate and handed her his. "Never let

Aurora Dove fill your plate. The woman doesn't believe in meat."

Summer followed Eben with her eyes as he walked to the food table and filled another plate. He knew! A gentle smile curved her lips as she bit into the fat, juicy hamburger.

Eben returned and took his place beside her. For the next several minutes, they ate and conversed pleasantly, at the same time listening to Mitzi flirt shamelessly with the congressman.

Summer bit the inside of her cheek to stop a laugh from escaping when Mitzi finally led the bedazzled congressman off.

"There goes your congressman," Eben said.

"He wasn't mine."

"No?"

"Naw," Summer answered. "I live in Iowa."

Eben got rid of their empty plates, then leaned back on his elbows and watched a group of men set up a badminton net. "Something has been bothering me for the past two days."

Summer studied a cluster of brown splotches on the toe end of her sneaker. For the past couple of days, something had been bothering her too. Somehow she didn't think Eben would bring up the subject of chemistry. "What's that?"

"Did you dream in color the other night?"

Summer glanced up at his sincere expression and grinned. He was curious! For all his narrow-mindedness about Champ he was willing to accept that a cup of tea could cause someone to dream in color. "What would you say if I said yes?"

He reached down and plucked a blade of grass. "I

would ask, How many times have you ever dreamt in color before?"

"And if I said never?"

"Then it must have been psychological. Aurora Dove said you would dream in color, so you did. It was the power of suggestion."

"And if I'd said that I dream in color frequently?"

"Then you obviously were having one of your frequent dreams."

Summer squinted up into the sun. Not one iota of gray in his thinking. Why should she bother to explain it to him? No matter what she said, he would figure it out logically and come up with an answer he could accept. She plucked a blade of grass and stuck it between her teeth.

"Aren't you going to tell me?" Eben asked.

"No." She chuckled at the look of astonishment on his face. "Why don't you ask Aurora Dove for a cup of tea and see for yourself? Some things in life should be experienced, not told about."

Eben frowned as he stared at a patch of blue sky framed by huge pines. Did he ever dream in color? He tried to think back to any of his dreams and couldn't remember. Wouldn't he remember if they had been in color? His eyes shone with excitement as he turned and looked at Summer. "You did, didn't you?"

Summer gazed into his eyes and groaned. They were showing signs of gray. She didn't want the gray that was seeping through. She was very comfortable with the Eben who knew exactly where he stood. He was an unimaginative perfectionist, and could be easily resisted. Any signs of being open-minded or willing to understand would be her downfall. She was sitting a thousand miles away from building a relationship.

Wanting to bring the conversation back to safer territory, she looked around at the unusual crowd and marveled again at the unique gathering. "Aurora Dove has a gift with people. Maybe the UN should employ her for peacekeeping missions."

Eben knew a change in conversation when it hit him. Why wouldn't she answer him? "I'll let you in on her secret. No one would dare misbehave for fear of hurting her feelings. Aurora Dove projects childlike innocence."

Summer turned her head and saw Aurora Dove reading the palm of a bearded giant dressed in black leather. "Is it an illusion?"

"I guess that depends on how you perceive her."

Curious, Summer looked at Eben. "How do you perceive her?"

Eben heard the challenge in her voice and knew he would cross the battle line if he answered truthfully. Aurora Dove had a heart of gold, but was made of steel. "I refuse to answer that question on the grounds that it would ruin a beautiful afternoon." They hadn't brought up the subjects of sea monsters, past lives, or perfect people, and as far as he was concerned, they shouldn't. He had learned a great deal about Summer in the past hour, all of it fascinating.

Summer chuckled. She was happy he hadn't answered. For the past hour they had been talking and getting to know each other. She was surprised and delighted by the man behind the perfect image. They shared a common love of old-time movies, both preferred reading to watching television, and each enjoyed being outdoors. "There's only one thing that could make this afternoon better."

"What's that?" he asked.

"Me beating you in a game of badminton."

Eben grinned wickedly. "I believe your day has just started to slide downhill."

Summer stood up and brushed crumbs off her lap. With a sigh she rubbed at a splotch of catsup on her white shorts. "Come on, smiley, put your racket where your mouth is."

Eben chuckled as he followed her over to the net and picked up a racket. "Being a gentleman, I'll let you serve first."

Summer wiped her forearm across her brow. The man was amazing; didn't he sweat? They had been playing in eighty-degree weather nonstop for the past twenty minutes, and Eben wasn't even breathing heavily. Her blouse was sticking to her back, and her left knee was skinned from when she had dived for the birdie. Eben looked as fresh and cool as he did when she first saw him at the barbecue. Life just wasn't fair.

Eben picked up the shuttlecock and bit back a smile. Damn, if she wasn't cute when riled. The score was tied at fourteen all; whoever got the next point would win the game. When he first agreed to play, he had planned on going easy on her, but he soon realized she was a fierce competitor. Letting her slide by would be an insult. If she won this game, she would have earned it. "Ready?"

Summer nodded and shifted her balance from one foot to the other. When the birdie came hard and fast to the left she was there to return it. She got ready to hit the next volley to Eben's weak spot—his backhand.

Eben tried to return the birdie, but it ended up tangled in the net. The lady was smart enough to pick up on his weakness and use it. He positioned himself to receive the serve.

"Ready?" She didn't wait for an answer. She fired the birdie across the net and was startled when it came back twice as fast. With no time other than to stick out her racket, she wasn't surprised when the birdie shot out of bounds.

Eben retrieved the birdie from under a pine tree and returned to the makeshift court. "Get ready, Summer, I'm firing this one in."

She was standing at the back of the court ready for anything, except what he served. The shuttlecock flew over the net and did a nosedive straight down. Summer didn't even have a chance to swing.

"That's game!" Eben shouted.

A group of teenage girls moved in and took the rackets. Summer walked off the court and pulled her shirt away from her back. "Good game, Eben." She quickly scanned his appearance for signs of exhaustion. There were none. "The last shot was brilliant. Where did you learn to do that?"

"It was the wind."

Summer gathered her damp curls in one hand to expose her damp neck. "Eben, there is no wind."

"How about I treat you to a nice cold soda?"

"Sounds great." Summer turned toward a path through the trees. "Meet me down by the lake."

Eben grinned at the streak of dirt across her bottom as she disappeared into the pines. Most women he knew wouldn't have played badminton with such zest, or be so nice about losing. Summer was turning out to be a great person; now if only she would forget her silly ideas about sea monsters. He headed for the sodas, whistling along with an old Jefferson Airplane tune that was blasting from a radio.

Summer sighed as she ran a cold, wet hand over the back of her neck. Heaven. She wiggled her toes on the rocky bottom of the lake, closed her eyes, and listened to the laughter and shrill cries of delight from the children nearby. This was what the Fourth of July was all about—freedom. Freedom to be with your friends or family. Freedom to be whoever you were, doing whatever you liked with whomever you wanted.

She reached down and gently splashed her arms with cool water. Why, when Eben admitted they had nothing in common and she'd confirmed it, did he seek her out? He was the one who joined her at lunch and hadn't left her side since. Not that she was complaining. Eben wasn't as bad as she had feared. He never mentioned Champ or the kiss they had shared.

She shielded her eyes and slowly searched the surface of the lake. Champ would not be spotted today. There had to be hundreds of boats and thousands of bathers in the lake. From most accounts, Champ was shy and stayed away from people and noise.

Eben walked to the edge of the lake and stopped to watch Summer. He shifted both cold cans to his left hand and picked up Summer's discarded sneakers.

He walked a few yards down the shore and sat down on a huge rock to wait.

Summer splashed water on the catsup spot and rubbed. When she was a child, her mother had called her hopeless and her father had constantly lectured her about her untidiness. At the age of twenty-six, she now understood that some people were neat, like Eben, and others should never wear white clothes. A chuckle escaped her throat as she envisioned herself in a white wedding dress. In all likelihood, the dress would be ruined before she made it down the aisle.

Summer jerked and turned around as freezing water pelted her back. A group of rambunctious boys were charging into the lake, splashing water everywhere. She laughed and shook her head. She scanned the shore, spotted Eben sitting on a boulder, and waved.

Eben waved back. She looked sexy as all hell with her damp curls bouncing every which way and the front of her blouse clinging to her moist body. He felt the sudden stirring of his body and cursed. Memories of the sweet, gentle kiss they shared filled his mind. He shifted his position as Summer slowly made her way back to shore.

He popped the top of a can of root beer and handed it to her. "I hope this is okay."

"It's fine." Summer tilted back her head and felt the cold liquid slide down her parched throat.

Eben's eyes followed a single drop of water as it traveled down her throat and disappeared into the shadow of her blouse. With a jerky movement he pulled the tab on his soda and gulped half the can.

Summer sat down next to him, brushed off her feet, and pulled on her sneakers. "The kids all seem to be enjoying themselves."

He glanced over at the screaming horde pushing their way in and out of the water. They reminded him of swarming bees. "Is that what your classroom looks like?"

"Lord, no. I don't allow bathing suits."

Eben chuckled. "I should have guessed." He watched as hassled mothers begged, pulled, and screamed at their youngsters to come out of the lake. There were too many people around. "Do you want to play a game of horseshoes?" He had helped Franklin set up the game earlier that morning and knew it was in the front yard, away from the crowd.

Summer cocked her head and considered the question. Yes, she wanted to play horseshoes with Eben. It didn't matter if he laughed at Champ—he was entitled to his own opinion–or that every spring she laughed at the filing instructions on her income tax forms. The IRS thought up more complex ways of saying the same thing over and over again. Today she wanted a friend. "Okay, you're on."

Summer studied the form of the older man named Bert as he tossed the horseshoe. It came flying toward her end of the court and landed a mere inch away from the stake. She leaned closer to Eben. "I think he's a ringer."

Eben chuckled. "A ringer is when the horseshoe circles the stake."

"I said *he* was a ringer, not the shoe." She watched as the second shoe came soaring. A dead ringer. "I hope when those two shysters conned you into us playing against them, you didn't bet any money."

Eben hid a smile behind his hand. Bert and Ernest

had been tricking innocent people out of their money since the day they were born twins, winning their father a bundle at thirty-to-one odds. If rumors could be believed, when they were sixteen they had pulled a sting operation against Capone and lived to tell about it. In their younger days they had dabbled in bootlegging, numbers, and the horses. They had retired four years before on their eighty-second birthday and supported themselves on harmless bets at horseshoes, pool, and any major sports event. "Why? Don't you think we could take them?"

Summer picked up her horseshoe, judged its weight, and pitched it toward the other end of the court. It landed two feet in front of the stake. "Does that answer your question?"

Eben kept his face blank. "You need to put a little more 'umph' behind it."

She carefully imitated Bert's motion and put a little more "umph" into the throw. Her warning cry broke the air just as the shoe smashed into Ernest's cane, four feet behind the stake. "Are you all right?" she asked.

A toothless grin appeared on his face as Ernest politely shook his head. Something that sounded like "dumb broad" reached her ears. She jerked her head up and studied the innocent expression on his wrinkled face. With a step toward Eben she whispered, "What did he say?"

Eben coughed and picked an imaginary speak of lint off his shorts. "I think he said he was fine." They watched as Ernest threw two ringers. Eben retrieved his shoe and explained to Summer every move he was making. She watched as the shoe went sailing through the air, clanged against the stake, and landed two inches away. His second shoe encircled the stake. "See how simple it is?"

Bert shuffled up to the shooting line, coughed twice, wiped his shaking hands down his trousers, took a deep breath, coughed again, and threw a ringer. He bent to pick up the other horseshoe and Ernest had to help him straighten back up. There was no way he could be in that bad a shape and still be beating the pants off someone half a century younger, Summer thought. His second toss landed an inch away from the stake. Summer groaned when Ernest called out the score. "Old geezers fourteen, young whippersnappers four."

To Eben she whispered, "How much money do you have riding on this game?" as she took her position at the line. She was concentrating on the distant stake when Eben's arms circled her from behind.

"No, you're holding the shoe wrong." He repositioned her fingers on the hard piece of iron.

Breathless, she asked, "What are you doing?"

Eben lightly pressed his lips against her ear and whispered, "Protecting my investment." He covered the fingers clutching the horseshoe and brought her arm back into the swinging motion. He followed the arm forward and instructed, "Release it here."

Summer felt the warmth of his body and breathed an "Ohhhh."

He released her hand and lightly hugged her. "Remember to concentrate on where you're throwing it."

Summer blinked at the stake forty feet away. Was he out of his mind? How was she ever going to concentrate on a hunk of metal sticking out of the ground when her stomach had just melted into her sneakers? She can not handle this. She had thought she could, but she couldn't. There was no way she could be just friends with Eben. The man's body didn't spell friendly; it shouted, *Dinner, come and get it!*

She glanced back at Eben and groaned at his encouraging smile. Her eyes narrowed when she saw Bert and Ernest cracking toothless grins and laughing at her. They thought she couldn't do it. Concentrating on the stake, she pitched the shoe. It landed leaning against the stake. "Look, Eben, I did it!"

"Always knew you could."

She inched her nose up in the air at the amazed toothless duo, and asked, "How much is it worth?"

"One point," Eben answered.

"Is that all? The ones that don't touch the stake are worth that much." She turned around and placed her hands on her hips. "I think it should be worth at least two points. Look at the way it's leaning. That was a difficult shot."

"Sorry, Summer, it's still worth only one point." He handed her another shoe. "Why don't you throw your other shoe and try for a ringer this time? That would be worth three points."

Eben missed her next throw, since he was too busy watching the enticing wiggle of her dirt-smeared bottom. How did she manage to get chocolate cake smudged on it also? He had been with her all afternoon and she hadn't touched any dessert.

Ten minutes later Summer glared at the geriatric duo as Eben handed them a ten-dollar bill. "You two should be ashamed of yourselves. Preying on unsuspecting victims," she admonished.

Bert croaked out a laugh. "Eben knew the odds. We play him every year."

"Hasn't won a game yet," Ernest wheezed as he poked his cane at Eben's foot.

Summer angrily turned to Eben as the chuckling due shuffled off in the direction of a young couple eyeing the horseshoe court. "You knew the whole time they were going to win?"

He grabbed her hand and led her away from the crowd. "No, I didn't know we would lose. I had no idea how well or how badly you played."

Summer stopped in the middle of the path. "I didn't play that badly."

"Of course you didn't. You were just a little rusty in the beginning." He reached over and rubbed a dusty smear off her cheek. "You even pitched a ringer."

Warmth spread across her cheek where his finger had touched it. Voices faded and a lone bird's song filled the air. "Why didn't you tell me?"

"Bert and Ernest support themselves by betting. Whenever possible I accept a wager and then let them win."

"You could have let me know."

"They like a challenge and deplore charity. They knew you were trying your best to win."

Summer frowned. "What would have happened if we had won?"

Eben's thumb rose to wipe the frown from her lips. "I would have made sure someone else placed a larger bet and lost."

He was flustering her again. These were not friendly, neighborly feelings dashing through her body. "You're a very nice person, Eben."

His thumb teased the corner of her mouth. He

wanted to kiss her. "Are perfect people allowed to be nice?"

Summer's startled blue eyes locked with his serious ones. Why was he going to ruin a wonderful afternoon? Her voice, when she spoke, was barely above a whisper. "Perfect people are always nice."

Eben's hand cupped her cheek, and his eyes held her gaze. "Then I should have allowed Bert and Ernest to lose?"

She shook her head slightly. "No."

"Summer, you're condemning me for something I don't understand. If I'm nice, I lose, and if I'm the villain, I lose."

Summer felt her back go up against an invisible brick wall. He was using logic again and twisting her words. "You're the one who said we're not compatible."

"I could have been wrong!"

The bricks started to dig in deeper. "Name one thing we're compatible in."

"Barbecues, hamburgers with the works, cold sodas, long walks on the beach, and being nice to two old men."

"Everyone does that."

Eben's hand slipped around her neck and pulled her closer. "Does everyone feel this?" He lowered his head to capture the astonished gasp on her soft lips.

Four

His lips had hardly brushed hers when he jerked back and glanced behind him. A yellow Frisbee landed beside him in a cloud of dust.

"Hey, mister, is your name Eben or Abner?"

Eben glared at the young boy waltzing up the path. He was wearing fuchsia knee-length shorts with turquoise alligators splattered over them. Orange high-top sneakers, without laces, flopped with every step he took, and a black ripped T-shirt with a bloody skull advertised a rock and roll band. Eben shuddered. This was what the youth of the nation looked like? These were the ones who would be paying his social security in his old age? "The name's Eben James."

"Yeah, you're the dude."

The boy picked up his Frisbee and waited.

Eben glanced at Summer, who shrugged, and looked back at the boy. "What's your name?"

"Harley."

"Harley?"

"Yeah." The boy kicked dirt into the air. "Mom promised Dad a brand-new motorcycle for Christmas, and instead he got me. I was born on December twenty-forth."

Eben was appalled. He scowled at the zigzags on the boy's shaved hair and the thin, straggly ponytail that hung a foot below his shoulders. A silver skull earring pierced Harley's right ear. What kind of parents would allow a boy to dress like this? The kind who named a little baby after a motorcycle, he answered himself.

Summer smiled at Harley. He obviously took a lot of ribbing about his name. "Hello, Harley. I'm Summer Hudson."

"Were you born in the summer?"

"No. I'm a March baby."

"Why did they name you Summer, then?"

"I don't know." Secretly she always wondered if her sensible parents named her after the season in which she was conceived. She dismissed the idea as being too sentimental for them. "I guess you can be thankful your mom didn't promise your dad a case of beer for Christmas?"

"Why? Because Bud is as bad as Harley?"

"I was thinking more along the lines of Moosehead."

Harley laughed. "Yeah, I never thought of it like that."

Eben gazed at the smiles curving Summer's and Harley's mouths. She understood this kid! His first reaction was to back away from Harley, but hers was to comfort him? "You were looking for me?"

"Yeah, my godmother says to tell you she needs the rest of the stuff and I have to help."

Baffled, Eben asked, "Who's your godmother?"

Harley rolled his eyes and looked at Eben as if he were from another planet. "Aurora Dove."

Eben's confusion vanished. "I forgot all about the food." He glanced at his watch and groaned. He saw Summer's curious look. "I have a bunch of food stored in my refrigerator. She was saving it for the dinner portion of the barbecue."

"I'll help you get it," Summer offered.

Eben smiled his thanks and turned back to Harley. "Go tell Aurora Dove that Summer and I will bring the food over."

"I'm supposed to help you."

He looked down at the boy and frowned. He didn't want to hurt his feelings, but he really didn't want a boy tagging along. He motioned the boy aside and slipped him two singles. "If you make yourself scarce, Aurora Dove would never know you didn't help."

Harley pocketed the bills, winked at Eben, and bowed toward Summer. "Hey, Ms. Summer, be thankful you weren't born on Thanksgiving."

"Why?"

"They could have named you Turkey."

Summer and Eben chuckled as Harley went wandering down the path, his laughter filling the empty spaces between the trees.

They left the rusty wagon at the bottom of the stairs and climbed to the deck. Summer turned to face the lake. Beautiful. The afternoon sun was still strong, making the water shine like a million sparkling diamonds. "How could you bear to leave it?"

Eben looked at the same view he had seen every day for the past three years. "Leave it?"

"To go to work, or to sleep, or food shopping."

He walked over to Summer and leaned against the rail beside her. He could pick out a dozen boats, and a water-skier still enjoying the afternoon. "A person has to make a living."

Summer turned and faced the back of the house. "Can you see the lake from every room?"

"No, just the living room, kitchen, and master bedroom." He pushed away from the railing and unlocked the sliding door. "My office, television room, and the two spare bedrooms all face the forest." He held the door open for her. "Do you want the nickel tour while we're here?"

With a forlorn expression she reached into her empty pockets and pulled them out. "I don't have a nickel on me."

Eben reached down and kissed the tip of her nose. "That was worth a nickel." He stepped back and allowed her to enter the kitchen.

Summer's eyes grew wide as she glanced around the spacious room. It was gorgeous. Exposed rustic beams supported the upper floor. The wall separating the living room and kitchen was painted a soft cream that complemented the pine flooring and cabinets. A braided blue oval rug was under a pine kitchen table and four chairs. Both the wall under the cabinets and the countertops were done in cobalt blue tile. Modern appliances blended in with the rustic, homey atmosphere.

She walked through the kitchen without saying a

word and entered the living room. She gasped when she saw the sliding glass doors and breathtaking view of the lake. Twin green plaid couches flanked a pine coffee table in the center of the room, and wooden stairs led up to the second floor. A huge massive stone fireplace nearly took up one wall. Logs were laid in, ready to be lit, and a silver-framed picture of an older couple sat on the mantel. "Your parents?"

Eben had been following her with his eyes as she walked toward the photo. "Yes."

She picked up the photo. "No brothers or sisters?"

"No, I'm an only child. My mother couldn't have any more after me."

"You don't have to apologize. I'm an only child too." She frowned as she took in the smiles on the couple's faces. They looked happy. "My parents didn't want any more after me."

He walked over to her and looked down at his parents. Did she see an ordinary middle-class couple or a couple still in love after thirty-five years of marriage? "On your Christmas list, did you write down 'baby brother' till you were sixteen too?"

Summer studied the woman in the picture and felt tears form in her eyes. That's what a mother was supposed to look like. There was a sincere smile on her lips and love and laughter in her eyes. The simple flowery dress made her look soft and approachable. Her own mother never wore flowery prints and was as soft as tungsten steel.

With trembling fingers Summer carefully placed the silver frame back on the mantel. "No, when I was four my parents explained that there wasn't a Santa

Claus." She turned and headed for his office. "After that I didn't see any need for Christmas lists."

Eben watched as she walked away. What in the hell was he going to say to her revelation? He wanted to apologize to her for what her parents had done. He wanted to take her in his arms, comfort her, and tell her that there really was a Santa Claus. Summer was an enigma. She didn't believe in Santa Claus, but was searching Lake Champlain for a sea monster. What was he supposed to make of that?

He glanced at his parents' picture and slowly shook his head. He couldn't imagine having the kind of parents Summer did. He positioned the picture back to its original place and followed her.

Summer's back was to the door, and she was staring off into the woods. Sunlight was filtering through the trees, lightning the forest floor. All the old hurt was safely buried by the time she heard Eben enter the room. "It's like living in two houses."

Eben bit back a groan. Why of all the women who had seen his home was Summer the one with the perception? Others had called his home rustic, quaint, and even charming. Summer had picked up on the vast differences in the same house. "Sometimes deer come right up to the windows."

She saw a chipmunk dart under a bush. "How do you choose?"

He didn't have to ask what she was talking about. He knew. "If I'm looking for serenity, I face the lake. If I want to be amused, fascinated, and kept on my toes, I sit in here or in the television room."

Summer turned away from the view. "Which way do you face most often?"

Eben's brows came together as he thought. "The lake."

With a nod of her head and a pensive look, she left the room. In most houses, the television room would be called the family room. But since he lived alone, he couldn't quite name it that. And it didn't hold just a television. It really was a high-tech entertainment room. A large-screen television, VCR, CD player, receiver, and speakers were placed around the spacious area. A brown leather couch was located for watching television or looking out the large picture window.

Summer completed the downstairs tour back in the kitchen, after locating two closets, a powder room, and a laundry room. "I must congratulate you on your magnificent home, Eben."

"Thank you, but don't you want the complete tour?"

Summer knew the upstairs contained his bedroom. The farther away from that kind of temptation she was, the better off she'd be. She didn't need to know what his bed looked like. He was already causing her to lose too many hours of sleep as it was. "Some other time." Like when she fully understood what was happening between them. "We better get the food over to the party before Aurora Dove passes out maps to the guests showing them where dinner actually is."

Eben chuckled. He wouldn't put it past Aurora Dove to pull such a number. The thought of two hundred people descending on his home caused a shiver to slide down his back. He opened the packed refrigerator and started to hand bowls to Summer. "Hurry up before they smell it."

When Summer passed Eben on the porch steps for the third time, she wondered how they were going to fit everything in one wagon. She entered his kitchen and glanced around. Spotless. The man either employed an army of housekeepers or didn't sleep at night. Countertops glistened, floors shone, and the stainless steel sink was actually stainless. She picked up the last two bowls and peeked in his trash can. It was empty! The man didn't even have garbage.

She walked over to the living room and looked around. No knickknacks cluttered the tables, no books left by a favorite chair, nothing. The only other picture in the room, besides the one of his parents, was an original watercolor hanging on the cream-colored wall. Soft blues and greens competed against light grays in the gentle, peaceful water of a lake. It was well done, obviously expensive, but she preferred the vivid oil painting of a bald eagle hanging in his office.

"Are you ready?"

Summer jumped. She hadn't heard Eben come up behind her. His arms slid around her and took the bowls from her hands. She could smell the faint aroma of his woodsy after-shave and feel the warmth of his body. She closed her eyes, breathed in deeply, and resisted the urge to press back into his arms. "Yes, the games should be starting soon, and I don't want to miss them."

She cast a last look at his living room. One glance at his immaculate house and then her well-lived-in apartment would tell anybody that they were utterly incompatible. So why was she disappointed that Harley had interrupted them?

• • •

Summer grimaced as a man stepped on her toe. Being a spectator was more dangerous than participating in events. She squeezed nearer to Eben and tried to get a better view of the few remaining contestants.

Eben pulled Summer closer and wrapped his arms around her waist. She leaned into him more, then burst into a gale of laughter. Aurora Dove, the bearded giant, and a man who appeared to be pushing ninety were tied for first place in the annual watermelon-seed-spitting contest.

Eben tightened his hold as the bearded giant roared his disappointment at being disqualified from the current round. "I can't believe Aurora Dove. She's never even entered the contest before, and this year she might win it."

Summer cheered Aurora Dove on. When the crowd quieted down, she tilted her head up and whispered, "Maybe she used to spit seeds in a previous life."

Eben groaned. "You can't possibly believe that!"

"Well, what else makes sense? You just told me she never did this before, and here she is tied for first."

He looked down into Summer's laughing blue eyes. Was she serious, or was she pulling his leg? He was having a great time with Summer and didn't want to spoil it by pointing out that there were no such things as past lives. "If Aurora Dove wins, I'll enter the three-legged race with you. But if she loses, you have to enter the egg toss with me."

Summer glanced down at her clothes and shook her head. Her coral-and-white-striped sleeveless blouse was wrinkled and smudged. The once-spotless white shorts probably were beyond cleaning and her sneakers were smeared with orange Jell-O, and she hadn't even eaten any. Eben's white shirt was still immaculate, and his khaki shorts weren't even wrinkled. How did he do it? "You know who's going to end up with egg all over herself, don't you?"

"Only if you don't catch it correctly."

A gentle sigh escaped Summer's throat as Aurora Dove was disqualified and the old man was declared the winner. Some days it didn't pay to get out of bed.

Eben bit his lip to keep back the laughter as he handed Summer another napkin. He watched as she wiped most of the gooey egg off her shorts and leg. Summer Hudson's legs in rolled-up jeans were fantastic, but in shorts they were dynamite. They were smooth, tanned, just as he had pictured them, and had yoke dripping down them. "Come on. Let's use Franklin's kitchen to wash that off."

Summer glared at him. "Why, don't you like flies buzzing around you?"

He quickly turned his laughter into a cough and pulled her into the house. After running a paper towel under the faucet he knelt in front of her.

Heat burned a path up her leg wherever the cool towel touched. She felt her heart start to pound and her breath come in hurried gasps. There it was again, that same attraction she had felt the other night. Only now it was hotter. His hand scorched her calf as he tenderly held her still. Her voice was low and jerky as she whispered, "I can do that."

Eben looked up from the shapely leg. Desire

throbbed throughout his body when he saw her eyes darken. "It was my fault for throwing it too hard."

She was breathless. "I should have caught it."

The cool towel traveled over her knee. "No, you should have told me you had never been in an egg toss before."

Summer stopped breathing as he wiped her trembling thigh. Lord, she felt hot.

Eben's hand tightened on the back of her knee as he finished cleaning her leg. Not a trace of egg was left on the dewy skin. He felt the slight tremor of her leg and closed his eyes.

The countertop bit into her hand as Summer grabbed it for support. Not sure if she was calling him in need, or pushing him away, she cried out his name. "Eben."

The slamming of the screen door broke the tension. Summer turned around guiltily and stared at Aurora Dove. Eben rose to his feet slowly, turned toward the sink, and proceeded to wet another towel.

"Did I interrupt something?" Aurora Dove asked cheerfully, looking at the two.

"No," Summer snapped. She pushed a bunch of curls away from her flushed face. "I mean, no, you didn't interrupt anything. I was just cleaning up from the egg toss."

Aurora Dove studied Eben's back and smiled. "Ah, yes, eggs can be such a sticky problem."

Eben muttered something indecipherable about sticky problems as he washed his hands for the third time.

Aurora Dove chuckled and headed for the refrigerator. "Chow's on again. You two better grab some dinner before there's nothing left."

Summer frowned and grabbed the wet paper towel from the floor, where Eben had dropped it. With more force than finesse she started to scrub the yellow stain on her shorts.

"She's gone," Eben said.

She continued to rub the spot.

Eben gently took the mutilated paper towel from her. "It will come out in the wash, Summer."

She felt humiliated as she looked out the window at the group of people crowding around the food-laden tables. What was wrong with her? She had never done anything like this before. A shudder slid down her spine at the thought of what might have happened if Aurora Dove hadn't walked in when she did. She had wanted Eben James! It didn't matter that they were at a barbecue with over two hundred people, hordes of screaming children, and blaring music. She had wanted him.

She needed to put some distance between them, and fast. "I think I'll call it an early night and head back to the cabin."

Eben understood her fear, because he felt it too. The attraction between them was growing. He always believed that a man could control his own destiny and emotions. The attraction he felt for Summer could be just as easily controlled.

Eben started to pick up the dirty paper plates that littered the kitchen, and dumped them in the trash. "If you leave now, you'll miss the highlight of the barbecue."

Curious, she asked, "What's that?"

He dumped a handful of plastic forks and spoons into the sink. "Fireworks."

Summer stopped her retreat. She loved to watch

fireworks. Maybe she was a little hasty in judging Eben's reaction. The man didn't look to be caught up in the throes of passion. He was cleaning up the kitchen, for cripe's sake. "Are they big fireworks?"

Eben breathed a sigh of relief. She wasn't going to leave. He began to pick up peanut shells that were scattered across the counter. "The city of Burlington sets them off over the lake."

"Can we see them from here?"

"If you'll join me for dinner outside, I'll personally guarantee you the best seat in the house."

Summer glanced down at her shorts and wondered if there would be enough time to change.

Eben read her mind. "If we eat now, you'll have time for a quick shower before the fireworks."

She rushed to the door and held it open. "What are you waiting for? Hurry up before Aurora Dove sees us and fills our plates with nutritious weeds."

Five

"Come in, the door is open," Summer shouted.

Eben opened the door and walked into the cabin. "Eben?"

He scowled in the direction where her voice came from—a closed bedroom door. With two hundred strange people running all over the place, she left her door unlocked and invited whoever was knocking to come on in. "Now's a good time to ask."

Summer glanced across the bedroom at the closed door as she finished tucking in the red silk blouse and snapping her jeans. He sounded annoyed. It wasn't her fault she wasn't ready yet. If he hadn't insisted on coming to pick her up, instead of her meeting him wherever, she wouldn't have had to straighten up the cabin. She quickly slipped her feet into a pair of sandals and threaded a belt through the loops on her jeans. "I'll be right out, Eben."

Eben looked around the small cabin in wonder. How could she have collected so much junk in the short period of time she had been there? Books, magazines, and telephone directories were stacked on the coffee table. Shelves flanking the fireplace were crammed with more books, newspapers, beach towels, and what appeared to be Christmas decorations. He slowly shook his head and glanced at the bedroom door again. "Don't hurry, we have plenty of time."

"Almost done."

He heard the hum of a hair dryer and sighed. Only Summer would consider soaking-wet hair almost done. He walked over to the kitchen area and glanced around. Dishes and bubbles filled the sink, the sugar bowl contained peppermint candies, and a green lace bra hung from a towel rack. Summer Hudson was disorderly, impulsive, and thoroughly intriguing.

Amused, he looked in the cabinets and refrigerator. Why would a woman buy two boxes of chocolate cupcakes and low-fat milk?

Summer finished applying mascara and added the final touch, a pair of dangling silver earrings. She critically glanced at herself in the bathroom mirror. This was as good as she got. Her cheeks were naturally tinted pink from the sun, the touch of eye makeup made her eyes seem bluer, and even her blond curls looked soft and controllable.

She wondered whom she was trying to impress. Eben was as different from her as caviar was from beer. The two together was inconceivable, but at least he would see her clean for once.

She opened the bedroom door and spotted Eben staring at the three-foot-high papier-mâché cow she had bought at a roadside stand while driving through New York. "Her name is Clementine."

Eben continued to gaze at the cow. "What is it?"

Surprised, Summer looked at the white and black animal. It looked like a cow to her; it even had pink udders. "It's a cow."

"I mean, what does it do?"

Puzzled, she said, "It stands there."

He turned and looked at her for a moment. "That's it? It doesn't do anything?"

Summer glanced from Eben's bewildered expression to the cow, and back again. "What do you want her to do—give milk?"

Eben's heart picked up a beat when he finally turned to the woman standing beside him. She was gorgeous. "No, I just thought it should be something."

She noticed his well-groomed appearance and damp hair. He cared enough about tonight's date to shower, change, and shave. "Well, sorry to disappoint you, but Clementine is nothing more than a cow."

"We'd better be going if we want good seats." He walked over to the door. "Bring along a jacket. It could get chilly later."

She quickly went into the bedroom and returned carrying an oversize off-white cardigan. She locked the door behind them and slid the key into the rear pocket of her jeans. "Where are these great seats anyway?"

Eben led her around the back of the cabin to a faint trail heading toward the lake. "You'll see when we get there."

She smiled her thanks as Eben took her hand and helped her over a cluster of tangled roots. The lake came into view between trees as they headed toward Eben's house. She guessed right; they were going to sit on his deck and watch the fireworks. So why did they have to hurry to get the best seats?

Summer lifted her brow in question when they headed toward the lake instead of the house. Understanding dawned as Eben led the way to a dock and a boat. Her voice held excitement as she looked at the small white craft. "We're going out on the lake."

Eben was glad he had rushed back from the barbecue to take the tarp off and ready the boat. The past years he had sat on his deck and watched the brilliant display from a distance. With Summer, it didn't seem enough just to watch the fireworks. He wanted to be there when they exploded and thousands of flickering colors floated gently downward. "Didn't I promise you the best seats in the house?"

He helped her into the boat and passed her a wicker picnic basket and an ice bucket with a bottle of champagne. "Do you mind holding the bucket while I drive?"

Summer glanced at the bottle. "Are we celebrating something?"

Eben untied the boat and hopped in. "The Fourth of July. You know, freedom, independence, Stars and Stripes forever."

She sat down and adjusted the ice bucket on her lap. "Do you do this every year?"

Eben turned the key in the ignition. No, I've never done anything like this before, and I have no idea why I'm doing it now, he thought. He shot her a quick glance and pushed the throttle forward. The boat took off across the lake. He had to shout above the roar of the engine to give her the only truthful answer he knew. "No, only when the mood strikes me."

Summer held the ice bucket with one hand and tried to keep her hair out of her eyes with the other. Excitement raced through her as she scanned the calm surface in front of them. What if Champ showed himself now? She hadn't brought her camera! Was the pounding of her heart caused by the legendary Champ, or by Eben? She cast a quick glance down at the picnic basket nestled between her feet and frowned. She'd bet next year's vacation to Scotland that in the basket were two crystal champagne glasses, crackers, and pâté, or possibly caviar. The setting was too perfect for anything less.

Eben eased up on the throttle as he approached the area where boats were gathering. He pulled back away from the crowd, turned off the engine, and dropped anchor. "We'll have a great view from here without cramping our necks." He switched on the running lights and took the ice bucket from her. "There's more room in the back."

Summer followed him to the rear and placed the basket on one end of the red bench seat and sat at the other. Was this how guys got girls in the back seat of a car, by promising them more room? She didn't know what game he was playing with his gourmet goodies, but she wasn't buying it. "This is a lovely boat. Did you just get it?"

Eben's lips curved up as he sat across from her and placed the ice bucket on the floor. Summer had just set the rules. "No, I bought it last year."

The western sky was blazing with the setting sun, and dozens of boats were drifting, zooming, or sailing across the lake. She shivered as a cool breeze stirred and the sun sank lower.

"Cold?"

She reached for her sweater and pulled it on. "A bit."

Eben stood, took the cushions off his seat, and lifted the wooden top. He pulled a plastic bag from the compartment and handed it to Summer. At her bewildered expression, he explained, "It's a blanket, in case you need it later."

Summer looked inside the white bag at the neatly folded plaid blanket and bit her lip. She had a plaid blanket in the trunk of her car for emergencies too. It had a grease spot, and one corner was stained from grape Kool-Aid. At that moment it was rolled into a ball and jammed under the spare tire to keep the tire from vibrating. She folded the plastic neatly around the blanket and sat it next to the hamper. "Thank you."

He watched as her glow faded and wondered if it was an illusion caused by the setting sun. He replaced the cushions and reached for the basket. A boyish smile teased his lips as he pulled two crystal glasses wrapped in white linen napkins. "Sorry, these are the closest things I had to champagne flutes."

Summer's eyes sparkled with delight as he revealed wineglasses. "It doesn't matter as long as we can drink from them."

"Wait until you see what else I packed." With boyish enthusiasm he pulled out a box of graham crackers shaped like teddy bears, ordinary crackers, and a can of cheese spread.

Summer fell back against the red cushions and laughed. He was serving junk food with imported champagne.

Eben frowned. What did she expect? Caviar and

pâté? There was nothing on this good earth that would persuade him to eat black fish eggs or goose liver. After witnessing her consume junk food at the picnic, he figured he'd be safe bringing the only junk food in his house. "What's so funny?"

She heard the hurt quality in his voice and immediately stopped laughing. "Absolutely nothing." She kicked off her sandals and tucked her bare feet under her. A gentle smile touched her lips. "Are you going to let the ice melt all over the bottom of the boat, or are you going to open the champagne?"

Eben read the message in her eyes and knew he had passed a test. With a flourish he wrapped a napkin around the bottle and started to wiggle the stopper. "Hold up the glasses, it's about to go."

Summer jumped as the stopper popped off and bubbly champagne gushed from the bottle. Her laughter mixed with his as they tried to capture the flowing liquid.

The last of the fading light dwindled as Eben stared at her exquisite smile. Twilight had come and gone and she hadn't once mentioned Champ. Was she finally realizing the foolishness of her quest? "The show should be starting soon," he said.

Summer could hear the shouting and laughter from the floating boats nearby. Champ had to be miles away from all this noise and excitement. "Where are they going to shoot the fireworks?"

His long, slim finger pointed above the gathering boats. "There, I think."

She frowned. "You won't be able to see from where you're sitting without breaking your neck."

"I'll manage."

"Don't be ridiculous. There's room for both of us on

this seat." She slid over. "Bring the crackers with you."

Eben didn't argue, and Summer leaned against his chest and looked skyward as a multitude of green sparkles exploded. A collective "Oohhh!" echoed across the water to mingle with her sigh.

The last glimmer of color was fading when a white flash exploded and a dozen rockets whistled in every direction, trailing multicolored sparkles. An awe-inspired "Ahhhh!" rose from the crowd.

Eben rested his chin on top of her curls and tightened his hold on her waist. He watched the glistening display and quietly oohed and ahad with the woman cradled against his heart. A glorious shower of gold twinkled against the blackened sky.

"Beautiful," Summer breathed.

He gazed down at her luminous face. "Yes," he whispered, "beautiful."

Summer sighed as the last ember of gold fizzled out. Why did it seem so natural to have Eben share this moment with her? When the first firework erupted, he'd shifted position and pulled her close, and she had gone willingly.

She watched as a burst of red filled the sky. The glasses and the graham crackers had done her in. When he had pulled them from the basket an amazing thing had occurred. She realized that she actually liked Eben as a person. Granted, she had been attracted to his good looks, fantastic body, and the impressive way he carried himself, but she hadn't particularly cared for the person underneath.

She took another sip of chilled champagne and tried to ignore the voice in her head saying she had never given him a chance. A shiver slid down her spine. What difference would it make whether she liked him or not? She wasn't into vacation flings.

"Cold?"

"No, someone must have walked over my grave."

Eben chuckled. "Now that's a cheery thought." Blue fireworks lit the sky. "The finale will be coming soon."

"How can you tell?"

"They're shooting them closer together. See how they're doubling them up?"

Summer sat transfixed as a burst of red lit the black sky, followed immediately by an explosion of white, and then blue. People in some of the surrounding boats applauded and shouted. She tilted her head back and gazed up at Eben. She didn't want the fireworks or this warm, content feeling to end.

Eben's heart slammed against his chest as the gleaming fireworks overhead were reflected in Summer's eyes. Lord, she was dangerous. He greedily followed the slow movement of her tongue as it moistened her lower lip. Her name emerged from his throat, half a curse, half a prayer. "Summer."

She shifted her weight and raised her mouth.

He captured her tempting lips with a hungry kiss. His tongue plunged into the sweet darkness of her mouth as fireworks exploded overhead. The distant shouts disappeared as her trembling fingers sank into his hair. A dreamy sigh escaped her as his warm hand slid under the cardigan to flatten against her silk-covered back.

Eben felt her response clear down to his toes. Her sweet tongue matched his every stroke. Heat flashed across his groin as her soft breasts pressed against his chest. Lord, he was burning up.

Summer tilted back her head and gasped for breath as Eben trailed fiery kisses over her jaw to lightly nip at the pulse throbbing beneath the satiny skin of her neck. She opened her eyes and peered up at the vibrant exploding sky. Greens, yellows, reds, and blues raged against the darkened heavens.

Her blood heated, and a warm sensation spread from her abdomen to settle between her thighs. Whistles, explosions, and the wild cheering from the boats went unheard as she directed Eben's mouth back to hers. Her eyes closed on the boisterous finale as deeper emotions erupted through her soul. She wanted Eben James.

Eben vaguely heard the thundering of the fireworks over the furious pounding of his heart. His hand slipped around and gently cupped the silk-covered breast. He captured her groan with his lips as his thumb stroked the hardened nipple. So responsive. So ready.

His fingers shook as they undid the top three buttons of her blouse and released the front clasp of her bra. The warmth of her skin burnt into his palm as he tenderly caressed the pale breast. He released her mouth and captured the protruding nipple with his lips.

Summer quivered as she arched her back and cried, "Eben." Where was this heat coming from? It wasn't supposed to be like this. A fiery liquid radiated from the junction of her thighs.

He heard her call his name and pulled the nub deeper into his mouth. He felt her body's response and turned his attention to the other breast.

Summer shivered with anticipation. Her hands tightened in his hair, and she pulled him nearer. She wanted him closer. The hard column of his arousal was pressed against her hip, and when she rubbed against him, Eben groaned.

His hand slid down her side to cup her hip. He pulled her closer to his pounding arousal and held her there. Desire and need throbbed in every nerve ending. He wanted her as he had wanted no other woman before. He raised his head, tenderly brushed back a wayward curl, and kissed her damp, waiting lips.

Reality interrupted as the distant sound of a boat starting up penetrated his desire-filled brain. What in the hell was he doing?

Summer moaned as his heated lips left hers. The warm pressure of his hand slowly released her hip to rest lightly on her waist. What happened? she wondered. She opened her passion-filled eyes and gazed at a flushed Eben.

"I'm sorry, Summer, that should not have happened."

She blinked and looked around. The sky was dotted once more with stars; not a puff of smoke remained from the impressive display of fireworks. Some boats were leaving, while others seemed to be continuing the celebration. Distant music, laughter, and the bang of ordinary firecrackers drifted on the evening breeze.

Mortified, she untangled her fingers from his hair and tried to bring her gaping blouse together. He tightened his hold.

"I brought you out here to see the fireworks, nothing else," Eben said. She felt his hold loosen and quickly redid her bra and buttons. "I guess the champagne wasn't such a good idea."

Summer glanced down at the ice bucket. Eben had one full glass, and her second glass was barely touched. The bottle wasn't even half-empty. She moved away from his warmth and pulled the sweater tighter around her. "One glass would not have swayed our judgment."

Eben ran a frustrated hand through his hair. How was he going to explain he still wanted her, but could not have her? How could he tell her about his principles? Sex, for the physical release alone, left him feeling empty and shortchanged. Since his college days, he had practiced the art of sharing both his body and mind with his special someone. So why was he ready to ditch every principle he possessed to have Summer?

Her face was exquisite in its innocence, her body possessed more curves than a knuckleball, and who would not like or respect a second-grade teacher? But dammit, she was searching for a sea monster! When the good Lord made Summer Hudson, he forgot to tighten all the screws.

He shifted his position, looked up, and sighed. "We missed the finale."

Summer backed farther away on the red-cushioned seat. The man reduced her to a mass of excited hormones with dynamic kisses and then wanted to discuss the scenery. Maybe it was the fireworks that set off the reaction between them when they kissed. There was something uncivilized and exciting about colorful bursts coming louder and faster until they reached a magnificent finale. Freud would have loved analyzing her parallel between fireworks and making love.

The sooner she put distance between Eben and

herself, the better off she'd be. He obviously was having a strange effect on her psyche as well as her body.

They hadn't missed the finale, they had experienced it. She lowered her feet and slipped her sandals back on, muttering, "Not necessarily."

Eben watched as she packed the basket and dumped the remaining champagne from their glasses overboard. She was calling it quits. It was the smartest thing to do. So why was his heart contracting in pain? In frustration, against his raging desire, he harshly muttered, "I wanted you."

Summer's head jerked up and she lost her balance. His hand shot out to steady her. "Relax, nothing is going to happen." He released his hold. "Contrary to popular opinion, most men don't go to bed with every available female."

Between clenched teeth, she ground out, "I think you better take me home, *now.*"

Eben ran his hand down his face and groaned. "I'm saying this all wrong."

Summer eyed the distance between them and the other boats. If she had to, she could swim it.

He quickly apologized. "I didn't mean to imply you were available." Eben could feel the tension radiating from her body. "You have to admit things were rapidly getting out of hand."

She'd sooner have leeches placed on her legs than admit the word "stop" never entered her mind while he was kissing her. "It was the fireworks."

"The fireworks?"

"They have this strange effect on me." It didn't matter if tonight was her first case of lust brought on by gleaming sparkles. There had to be a reasonable explanation for what she felt in Eben's arms, and as far as she was concerned, she was placing the blame on the Declaration of Independence.

Eben stared at Summer's stubborn expression. A hesitant "Oh" emerged from his parched throat. Was she serious? Firecrackers turned her on! When he had taken her in his arms, he had forgotten that fireworks were exploding above their heads. He'd also overlooked the fact they were sitting in an open boat in the middle of Lake Champlain with hundreds of boats surrounding them. They would have had more privacy in Aurora Dove's kitchen.

He felt something he hadn't felt in a long time— challenged. It was like the feeling he got every November, when the new tax laws came out. After years of studying and working with the same old laws, it was a challenge when new ones were initiated and he had to match wits against the big guys to find his clients honest tax breaks. Over the years, he had encountered and avoided many gray areas in accounting. All his clients' returns were done honestly and to the best of his ability, without overstepping into the questionable gray areas. Eben James had the reputation of never having had a client audited by the Internal Revenue Service.

Was Summer herself one of those gray areas she warned him about? How could she attribute what had just happened to fireworks? It was mutual desire, not colored gunpowder, that had ignited the fire between them. Fascinated by the challenge she'd just issued, he asked, "Would you have dinner tomorrow night with me?"

"What?"

"I can pick you up around seven. There's a nice

lakefront restaurant in Pine Harbor that serves some of the best seafood around."

Shocked, she asked, "Why?"

Good question, he thought. "I would like to get to know you better."

"Before what?"

"Before you return to Iowa, Summer. Nothing more." He cocked his head and wondered about her defensiveness. "I had the feeling something special was happening tonight between us. With your fetish for fireworks, I guess I was wrong."

Summer silently groaned. He thought she had a fetish for fireworks.

"I'd like the chance to get to know you without all the excitement of whistling rockets and exploding colors," he said.

She ran her finger over the fine crystal glass still in her hand. Eben James wasn't perfect. Her parents would have been appalled at the thought of serving graham crackers in the shape of animals with French champagne. She carefully wrapped the glasses in a linen napkin and placed them in the basket.

Eben was gorgeous to look at, could hold an intelligent conversation, and at times showed a sense of humor. The deciding factor was that he was a gentleman. She was thankful he had called a halt to their heated kisses, even if his reason was still unknown. What would one dinner hurt? "Seven o'clock would be fine."

He smiled. "I better get you home before the partiers start their boats and pick the least drunk person to drive them."

The return trip was made in silence. Eben docked the boat and securely tied it for the night. He took the basket, empty ice bucket, and half-filled bottle of champagne from Summer and placed them on the dock. With gentlemanly concern he helped her from the boat.

From the pocket of his windbreaker he pulled out a flashlight. His warm hand reached out and held one of her daintier ones as he started to lead the way down the beach toward the path they had used earlier.

Summer glanced around into the darkness. The woods that had seemed so peaceful in the daylight now looked menacing and sinister. "Will you be able to find the path?"

Eben shone the light toward a huge crooked pine tree. "It's right there."

Summer gripped his hand securely as he ducked under the branches and blackness surrounding them. In the distance she could hear the muffled shouts of Franklin and Aurora Dove's guests. She heard a car door slam, a motorcycle start up, and in one of the cabins a baby was crying. All sounds of human occupation. So why did she feel isolated and alone with Eben? More importantly, why was there a warm, secure feeling radiating from their clasped hands?

Eben led the way along the same path he had followed home the night he had kissed her. So much had changed since then; so much had stayed the same. He had desired her from the first night spent in the raft. Only now he wanted more than just a willing body, he wanted to understand the entire woman.

In silence he played the light across the wooden

steps of her cabin and climbed up to her porch. "You should have left the light on."

Summer dug the key out of her pocket. "It wasn't dark when we left." She inserted the key, twisted the knob, and opened the door. With a flick of her wrist she turned on the yellow bug light hanging above the door. "Thank you for the lovely evening, Eben." Not knowing what else to say, she added, "I never watched fireworks while drinking champagne before."

He smiled at her golden complexion gleaming in the amber light. "Neither had I." His eyes focused on the lush fullness of her lower lip. "Make sure you lock the door this time."

Her lips pouted. "I've taken care of myself for years. I don't need another father."

"I have no intention of becoming a father figure to you, Summer. I'm just worried for your safety, that's all. Franklin and Aurora Dove had all kinds of people floating around here today."

"And they were all nice."

"Yes, they were." Eben sighed. "Please, lock the door for my peace of mind."

"Eben, I always lock my door at night."

The sweet temptation of her curving lips was too hard to resist. He bent and captured the smile.

Summer's arms rose to encircle his neck as she surrendered her lips. Warmth flowed through her as his arms tugged her closer. It was happening again! He touched her and she went up in flames. This wasn't just chemistry, it was anatomic transformation!

A purr of satisfaction twisted in her throat as his tongue swept across her lower lip and slid into her mouth. She enticed his tongue in farther with a gentle swipe of hers.

Eben tried to draw a deep breath as her hips gently rocked against his arousal. He was beginning to feel like the fireworks she claimed to be so fond of. All he needed was a label across his libido that read Danger, Highly Explosive.

He pulled his mouth away and stepped back. It was all happening too fast again. "I'll pick you up at seven tomorrow night."

She blinked. He was the one to end it again. Words failed to emerge from her throat, so she nodded her head.

Eben walked over to the steps. "Good night, Summer."

As he faded into the trees she whispered, "Good night, Eben."

"Summer?"

Her eyes squinted as she tried to see into the darkness. "Yes?"

"You were wrong."

"About what?"

"How do you explain your reaction this time, Summer? The only fireworks exploding were coming from us."

Six

Summer felt the warmth of Eben's hand on her back as they followed the maitre d' to their table. Pine Harbor Inn was an old stone building with additions built on over the years. Dining tables were placed throughout several gracious Victorian-style rooms. Ceilings soared to over ten feet in height, ornamental fireplaces dominated each room, and the pine flooring was aged by the passage of time. The soft melody being played on a piano drifted over the elegant diners.

A sigh of enchantment left Summer's lips as they were shown to their table. "It's beautiful."

Eben smiled. "I knew you would like it."

She glanced from the white marble fountain gracefully trickling in the center of the room to the white ceiling fans circulating cool air so that the heat pouring in from the dozens of windows wasn't so oppressive. Huge palms, ferns, and blooming gardenias formed natural dividers between the tables to ensure privacy. It was romantic and secluded, the *perfect* restaurant.

Summer looked away from Eben and stared out over the lake. She was doing exactly what she had promised herself she wouldn't do. She was comparing Eben to her parents and Richard. Today she had traveled past Plattsburgh to visit a sight where Champ had been spotted previously. While sitting on the shore, she had studied the smooth surface of the lake and had run the previous night through her mind for the fifth time.

She had wanted Eben, physically and emotionally, and Lord help her, she hadn't cared that they were in his boat! Where had the refined, demure lady her parents tried to raise disappeared to? She had been attracted to men before, but never with the intensity that Eben created. With Richard, her ex-fiancé, she had experienced the sparks; with Eben it had been the heated embers of desire. She had wanted to stoke those embers into a blaze.

Somewhere during the long, sleepless night and the hours of staring at a calm lake, she had realized she was not giving Eben a fair chance. Who was she to condemn him if his house was spotless—wasn't that considered an admirable trait? What sane woman went looking for a slob? What sane woman would be contemplating an affair with a man she had known less than a week?

A shiver slid down her back. She had finally admitted to herself why she had taken such care in dressing for tonight's dinner date. She had wanted to prove to Eben she didn't always look as though she collected waste for a living. After returning to her cabin hours before it was necessary, she had cleaned up the mess from breakfast and swept armloads of newspapers and magazines into boxes and stacked them neatly in a corner. As a final act of cleanliness, she had washed the dishes that had been soaking in the sink for the past two days.

With the cabin put in order, she had headed for the bathroom and emptied every drop from the hot water heater into the tub. Two hours later, on the precise stroke of seven, she had stood in the living room answering Eben's knock. The look on his face had been worth every effort that had gone into her organized attack against the clock. For the first time in her life, she had been ready when a date came to pick her up.

Her mother would have disowned her if she ever found out what she had done to the basic black dress she had given her last Christmas. Somewhere back in Iowa was the stylish jacket that was supposed to be worn with the dress. Summer preferred a shocking pink shawl, with metallic silver threads running through it, to wrap around her shoulders. A matching wide pink belt replaced the original nondescript black one. Silver necklaces draped her throat, and a pair of silver hoops swung from her ears.

A ghost of a smile touched Summer's lips as she looked out over the shimmering lake. It was a real shame she had forgotten to put on her shoes before she had opened the door to Eben's knock.

She looked away from the lake and studied the enchanting view. Sparkling white lights lit the promenade along the lake. A formal garden, complete with white wrought-iron benches, towering hedges, and flowing fountains, stood between the restaurant and Lake Champlain.

Eben looked out of the restaurant window and wondered what was holding Summer's attention. She was so lovely tonight. He had noticed the looks of appreciation and envy other male patrons cast their way as they walked to their table. An unjustified sense of pride had tilted his chin up a notch. When she had opened her door to him earlier that night, he had felt as if someone had punched him. If she was attractive and charming in shorts and jeans, she was devastating in a dress. The fact that she had forgotten to put on her shoes only enhanced her charm.

"Can we walk out in the garden after dinner?"

Eben forced his mind away from the mental picture of Summer's legs. "If you like. I was hoping we would go dancing in the lounge, though."

The prospects of being held in Eben's arms while gently swaying to a slow beat was too good to pass up. "How about we compromise and do both?"

The dimly lit private garden with its hidden paths and secluded benches held great appeal. His hand reached out and tenderly covered one of hers. "We could always go dancing some other night."

Not on your life, she thought. "No!" A tide of pink swept up her cheeks. "I mean, dancing sounds wonderful."

Eben was speculating on the reason for her blush when he was interrupted by the waiter. They ordered, and when the food and wine came, Eben saw no reason to be disappointed.

Summer swallowed a mouthful of trout and took a sip of wine. The label on the bottle sitting in the ice bucket boasted a name and date that would have made her father sit up and salivate. The meal was superb, the conversation stimulating—when she remembered to open her mouth to participate. So why was she hurrying through the meal?

The soft murmuring of the other diners faded, leaving Eben and Summer in their own private world. They lightly discussed politics and art—their opinions differed—and the intricate workings of Summer's toaster, which had set the toast on fire that morning. They agreed that Eben would look at it later.

Summer felt the air between them heat up with excitement, anticipation, and something primitive that had nothing to do with toasters or politics. She picked the almond slices out of her string beans and ate them. She should have worn something cooler. Her shawl was draped over the back of the chair, and her breathing was short and shallow. Lord, it was hot in here. She could feel the weight of her dress against her breasts and the silky friction of nylons rubbing against her inner thighs.

Eben wondered if he would make a fool out of himself if he asked the waiter to turn up the air-conditioning. It was getting awfully uncomfortable in there. The setting sun that was transforming the lake into a shimmering blazing inferno wasn't the only spectacle. If he stood up, his obvious condition would be noticeable not only to Summer but to every other diner in the room. With a muttered curse he speared his green beans. Great! Now he couldn't even have dinner with Summer without becoming aroused. Anyone listening to their conversation could see how much they didn't have in common. Yet he still wanted her.

"What do you think of Styrofoam?"

Eben's fork paused in midair. "Styrofoam?"

Passion awaits you...
Step into the magical world of

Loveswept

E N J O Y . . .

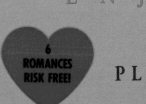

6
ROMANCES
RISK FREE!

PLUS

FREE GIFT

etach and affix this stamp to the
reply card and mail at once!

Enjoy Kay Hooper's *"Larger Than Life"*!
Not for sale anywhere, this exclusive
novel is yours to keep–FREE–
no matter what!

S E E   D E T A I L S   I N S I D E ...

A Magical World of Enchantment Awaits You When You're Loveswept!

Your heart will be swept away with Loveswept Romances when you meet exciting heroes you'll fall in love with...beautiful heroines you'll identify with. Share the laughter, tears and the passion of unforgettable couples as love works its magic spell. These romances will lift you into the exciting world of love, charm and enchantment!

You'll enjoy award-winning authors such as Iris Johansen, Sandra Brown, Kay Hooper and others who top the best-seller lists. Each offers a kaleidoscope of adventure and passion that will enthrall, excite and exhilarate you with the magic of being Loveswept!

- ♥ *We'd like to send you 6 new novels to enjoy—<u>risk free!</u>*
- ♥ *There's no obligation to buy.*
- ♥ *6 exciting romances—plus your <u>free gift</u>—brought right to your door!*
- ♥ *Convenient money-saving, time-saving home delivery!*

Join the Loveswept at-home reader service and we'll send you 6 new romances about once a month— <u>before they appear in the bookstore!</u> You always get 15 days to preview them before you decide. Keep only those you want. Each book is yours for only $2.25*. That's a total savings of $3.00 off the retail price for each 6 book shipment.

*plus shipping & handling and sales tax in NY and Canada

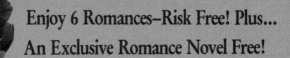

Enjoy 6 Romances–Risk Free! Plus...
An Exclusive Romance Novel Free!

Detach and mail card today!

Loveswept

AFFIX RISK FREE BOOK STAMP HERE.

Yes! Please send my 6 Loveswept novels RISK FREE along with the exclusive romance novel "Larger Than Life" as my free gift to keep.

RA   412 28

NAME

ADDRESS   APT.

CITY

STATE   ZIP

MY "NO RISK"
Guarantee

I understand when I accept your offer for Loveswept Romances I'll receive the 6 newest Loveswept novels right at home about once a month (before they're in bookstores!). I'll have 15 days to look them over. If I don't like the books, I'll simply return them and owe nothing. You even pay the return postage. Otherwise, I'll pay just $2.25 per book (plus shipping & handling & sales tax in NY and Canada). I *save* $3.00 off the retail price of the 6 books! I understand there's no obligation to buy and I can cancel anytime. No matter what, the gift is mine to keep–*free!*

SEND NO MONEY NOW. Prices subject to change. Orders subject to approval.

"White resilient polystyrene plastic shaped like little peanuts."

"Ah." Eben smiled. "An environmental question." He knew they would meet on middle ground on this topic. The previous month he had written out a check to Greenpeace.

"Do you buy dolphin-safe tuna?"

Eben chuckled. She was reaching for a way to defuse the sexual tension between them by starting an argument. "Sorry to disappoint you, Summer, but I even turn the water off while brushing my teeth."

Summer stared down at her half-eaten dinner. Life would have been simpler if Eben's idea of a fun time was to go clubbing baby seals to death.

After their meal was taken away, Eben led her to the dance floor. A soft, sensual melody wove its way around them and the handful of swaying people. Eben tightened his hold on Summer, and several tunes later, he maneuvered them into the shadows. Desire was pounding through his body with every beat of his heart. Taking a deep breath, he whispered, "Summer?"

Summer opened her eyes and rubbed her cheek against the lapel of his suit jacket. All she would have to do was tilt her head up slightly and she would be able to kiss his tempting lower lip. "Hmmm."

The gentle whisper of her breath feathered over his jaw. If he didn't get out of there now, he'd end up doing something incredibly rash, like slamming the lid down on the baby grand piano and ravishing her to a tempo created by Gershwin. "Would you like to take that walk now?"

Three slow, lingering songs earlier she might have been able to get her legs to cooperate, but now they were mush. She slipped her hands under his jacket and ran them up his back. Firm muscles contracted under her fingers. She raised her head and gazed up. "Can we stay a little longer?"

He kissed the end of her nose and pulled her closer. He would have given her the moon had she asked. "As long as you like."

Summer breathed a sigh of relief and snuggled closer. She closed her eyes and concentrated on the scent of Eben's after-shave. Weeks from now, when she was back home in Iowa, she wanted to be able to close her eyes and relive this moment.

Eben inhaled the cool evening air and prayed it would drop his body's temperature and lessen his arousal. One thing was for certain, he had to get Summer out of the secluded garden. "There's a gate over here that leads to Crafter's Alley."

She pulled the shawl around her shoulders and glanced in the direction he indicated. "Crafter's Alley?"

"It's the name of the promenade in front of the shops on the shoreline."

She cast a wishful glance at the path that led to the gazebo. "The shops aren't open now, are they?"

Eben knew she was hooked. There wasn't a woman alive who could resist shopping. "No, but the display windows are kept lit so you get tempted enough to want to return." He walked over to a white picket gate and held it open.

Summer bit back a silent moan. She was not forward enough to ask Eben to stay in the garden with her. She reached for his outstretched hand and stepped into the light. "That sounds lovely."

Twenty minutes later Eben was convinced something was wrong. Summer had gazed into the windows of about ten stores, and the only comment she had made was about a kite for her class and a lesson in aerodynamics. She had literally set the record in bypassing a jeweler's display window.

He glanced around at the people strolling by. A fat bald man was dragging a reluctant bulldog, and three elderly ladies were chattering loud enough to be heard halfway down the Alley. A shudder slid down his spine at the sight of a young couple necking on a bench. What had happened to his romantic evening with Summer?

Summer stopped in front of the window of the local gallery. Eben took a step forward and studied the canvas that caught her eye. Fog swirled and danced across the surface of a lake while the first blushing rays of morning streaked the sky behind a harsh mountain range. It was both powerful and gentle. It held hidden darkness and eternal light. The artist had captured the magic of twilight on canvas.

He wrapped an arm around Summer's shoulder and pulled her close. "You like?"

Who wouldn't be drawn to such an intense painting? she thought. She gazed down at the discreet price tag and sighed. A quarter of her yearly income for one picture. She was better off sticking to the framed posters and reprints that decorated her apartment. "The artist is very talented."

Eben watched as Summer walked away and casually glanced at the mannequins in the window of an exclusive boutique next door. With a frown he threw the painting a last look and joined her.

Three stores later he had had it. Something was not right. He was about to ask Summer what was wrong when a group of teenage boys came staggering down their side of the walkway. With a groan of frustration he grabbed her elbow and marched her over to the opposite, less trafficked, side, away from the window displays.

Summer gasped in surprise. What was his problem now? She had meekly followed his lead and cooled the tension that had been racing between them. She had thought of aerodynamics lessons and paintings she couldn't afford. Anything but what was going on between them. She was angry with herself. She hadn't had the gumption to initiate a romantic stroll through the empty gardens. Her parents' preaching of proper behavior for a lady had sunk in deeper than she had thought.

Eben backed her up against the railing that separated the pavement from the beach. He looked down into her bewildered face and tenderly brushed a golden curl away from her eye. It wasn't her fault the evening was rapidly dying. The fire that had been kindled when he had opened her cabin door had flared during dinner. It had roared out of control while he tightly held her and they danced. He had tried to control the flames by taking away the temptation of the garden before they were both consumed. "What's going through your mind?"

Summer felt the warmth of his fingers and shivered.

"Cold?"

She shook her head and tried to read the expression in his eyes. "No."

"Do you want to tell me what's bothering you?"

How did a lady say she wanted what his body had promised while dancing without sounding like the town slut? She had never been aggressive or seductive before. Why didn't he just kiss her, and she could show him what she wanted? A gentle breeze softly tossed her golden curls as she remembered a story she had read to her class in which the moral was that first steps are usually the hardest. She clasped her trembling fingers in front of her and took her first tentative step. "A walk in the garden would have been nice."

Eben's grip tightened on the railing on either side of her as his gaze traveled up from her trembling lower lip to her huge anxious eyes. "The first dark, isolated spot we ran across I would have kissed you."

A hint of a smile touched her lips. "I know."

He sucked in a breath and forced his hands not to reach for her. "Something extraordinary happens every time I kiss you. I'm not sure I can control it any longer."

Their gazes locked, and her smile grew. "I'm not asking you to."

His knuckles turned white from clenching the rail. She was serious. It was evident in the depths of her eyes. He moved closer and released the railing. Lightly cupping her delicate jaw, he tilted her face upward. He was about to capture her smile when loud laughter erupted from the teenagers. With a muttered curse he suppressed the desire. "Will you come home with me tonight?"

The gritty texture of his voice and his heated gaze

caused liquid fire to swirl low in her abdomen. Here it was, handed to her on a silver platter, and she didn't have to ask. Her answer was thick with desire. "I thought you'd never ask."

Eben raised his face to the evening sky and released the breath he had been holding. Now all he had to do was drive them both home without wrecking the car. "I don't see any."

Bewildered, she looked up at the sky. "Any what?"

"Fireworks." Eben chuckled, remembering last night.

With a touch of the devil, she said, "Maybe they'll appear later."

Eben's laughter faded as he looked down at her. "Indubitably."

Eben yanked his tie loose and turned on another light. "Would you like something to drink?"

Summer nervously played with the fringed edge of her shawl. "Something cold would be nice." She glanced around his living room and wondered what she should do now.

He watched her fingers tangle, pull, and mutilate the metallic threads. What did she think he was going to do? Hustle her up to the bedroom before she changed her mind? "Why don't you go into the other room and see if there's any music or video you would like to put on?"

When she nodded, he turned and walked to the kitchen.

Moments later he carried two tall glasses of soda into the room and chuckled. Summer was muttering dark threats to his sound system and questioning his CD player's parentage. "Can I be of assistance?"

"How does this thing work?" There were enough red, green, and amber lights on the stereo that it could pass for a Christmas tree. "I've pressed every conceivable button there is, but it still won't take the disc."

He placed the sodas on coasters and pressed every button but two. He gently slid the disc in and turned the volume down so it wouldn't rattle the windows. Sultry notes filled the room. With a bow he held out his hand. "May I have this dance?"

With a gentle swish of her dress she moved into his embrace, and for the second time that evening her voice thickened. "I thought you'd never ask."

The first strain of music had barely faded when he reached down and cupped her chin. "You are beautiful," he muttered against her trembling mouth.

The shawl slowly floated to the floor when she raised her arms to encircle his neck. Hunger racing through her, she opened her mouth and yielded its treasures to Eben. Hard hands pulled her closer to his warmth. She needed more. With trembling fingers she pushed his jacket off his shoulders and down his arms.

Eben broke the kiss to shrug out of his jacket. He ran a hand over the gentle swelling of her buttocks, up her waist and back, to tangle in the three silver necklaces adorning her throat. "Don't move," he whispered against her neck as he started to undo each of the strands.

Summer shivered as his lips moved down her arced throat, only to be halted by the barrier of her dress.

Her hands clenched his shirt when he dropped the strands of silver on the coffee table.

"I told you I wouldn't be able to control myself." Eben's voice was deep and uneven. "I'm not sure we're even going to make it upstairs."

A beckoning smile curved Summer's lips as she walked backward toward the doorway. Eben pulled off his tie and followed her into the hall.

Summer halted, took her earrings off, and laid them on a small table. She studied the heated flush staining Eben's neck. "Did I ever tell you how wonderful your kisses taste?"

Eben reached for her and groaned. "Now I know we aren't making it up those stairs." His mouth sealed her protest.

Summer felt herself being lifted up against his arousal and kicked her shoes to the floor. Her breasts ached with need and her fingers explored the rigid muscles straining in his back.

He held her off the ground, pressed up against him, and walked to the stairs. Summer pulled the annoying shirt out of his pants and ran her hands up his heated back. When he stopped at the bottom step, her fingers trembled trying to undo the stubborn row of buttons.

Her pink belt landed on the first step. His shirt was draped over the banister. Without releasing her mouth, he slowly lowered the zipper of her dress. Summer's fingers tunneled into the soft curls covering his chest.

Eben felt the heat of her fingers and moaned as desire tightened his arousal. It was too much, too soon. He trailed a path of feverish kisses across her jaw and lightly nipped her small pink earlobe. "You might have to help me up."

Summer chuckled and moved up a couple steps, running her tongue over her lower lip, and decided to try to walk.

Eben's hand shot out and grabbed the banister for support as he watched her small pink tongue spread a dewy sheen over her lower lip. Golden curls danced with each step she took, and the black dress swirled enticingly around her knees. He was bewitched. He was enthralled. Could he be in love?

Summer stopped on the top step and gazed down at Eben. He looked as though he were experiencing the shock of his life. "Eben?"

He shook his head to clear it, then took a step toward her. "You're beautiful." Another step. "You have a great sense of humor." He took off a shoe and dropped it as he climbed another step. "You are intelligent." His other shoe was abandoned on the next step. "You're caring and responsible."

Their gazes locked as he continued to climb. His socks were tugged off and dropped. She enticingly raised her skirt a few inches and unfastened a silken nylon. With meticulous care she slowly pulled the stocking down her thigh, over the shapely calf, and off her slender foot, before draping it over the railing.

Eben stopped breathing as she repeated the performance with the other leg. He gazed wishfully at the nylons. "I could have done that."

A purely feminine smile lit her face. "I'll remember that for the future."

He climbed the remaining steps and stopped just below her. "I'll hold you to it." He reached out and carefully lowered the straps of her dress.

Summer stepped out of the pool of black and impatiently kicked it aside. She stood proudly but hesitantly in a black half-slip and a black strapless bra.

Eben sucked in his breath. "I take it back, you're not beautiful, you're exquisite."

Summer reached out and ran the back of her fingers down his jaw. "So are you." His hand captured her fingers and brought them up to his mouth. She started to tremble as he seized each finger with his lips and ran his tongue over the sensitive pads. Her knees gave out when he playfully nipped the base of her thumb.

He swept her up into his arms and carried her down the hall to the master bedroom. Moonlight illuminated the king-size bed, making it seem a sensuous island. He allowed her legs to slide downwards until she was standing by the foot of the bed.

Summer's breath caught in her throat as Eben's fingers traced her collarbone. A purr of satisfaction escaped her lips when the bra fell to the floor.

With pleasure he slowly skimmed his hands from her waist, up over her ribs, to tenderly cup the rose-tipped breasts. His breath was warm as it feathered over a protruding nub. "Gorgeous."

He gently pulled the sensitive nipple into his mouth, and she arced her back and dug her fingers into his shoulders. Moisture and need gathered at the junction of her thighs. Summer closed her eyes and thrust her hips forward. The fog of desire that surrounded her made coherent speaking impossible. In a desperate attempt to make him understand, she called his name. "Eben!"

Heated hands rapidly slid the silken slip down her

hips as he kissed the last traces of his name off her quivering lips. She kicked the slip away and sank into his embrace.

The feel of her moist nipples burrowing into his chest sent the last of his control flying. He picked her up and laid her across the bed, then gazed at the paleness of her breasts and the tantalizing darkness of her kiss-swollen nipples. Eben gulped in air as his gaze moved downward. A black garter belt and panties were all that stood between him and heaven.

Summer's eyes followed his hands as he undid his belt and impatiently pushed underwear and pants down in one swift movement. Lord, he was splendid! She watched the harsh rise and fall of his chest, the slight quivering of anticipation in his taut muscles. He was rigid with desire. Desire she shared. With awe she reached out a hand and whispered, "Magnificent."

The mattress dipped slightly as Eben joined her. His mouth fused with hers, and ardent hands caressed and stroked her responsive breasts. A cry vibrated in her throat when his thumb gently flicked the hardened nipple. With more zealousness than skill she ran her fingers down his back and attempted to pull him closer.

Eben's mouth left hers to trail a string of moist kisses down her neck. "Easy love, we have all night." He brushed a kiss on each rosy-tipped breast as he knelt over her. His hands shaking with restraint, he peeled the last silken barrier down her graceful legs.

Summer's unsure hands fell by her sides and clutched the bedspread. A soft kiss landed on her ankle. "Eben?"

"Shhhh" was whispered against her slightly bent knee.

Sensations soared to a feverish pitch. Summer's head rolled from side to side. "Please . . ."

Eben lifted his mouth away from a highly sensitive spot on her inner thigh. "Please what?"

"Make love to me."

The pleading sound of her voice tore at his heart. He shifted position, rising above her on his elbows. He was tempted to turn on the light when he couldn't interpret her expression in the dim room. "Summer?"

"Now, Eben, please." Summer raised her hips and grazed the tight curls covering her womanhood against his throbbing member. She opened her thighs wider when he sucked in a breath. "I've wanted this since last night."

Eben's forearms shook and his teeth bit into his lower lip as he slowly sank into the hot, sweet, moisture of Summer. Uncertainty crossed her pleasure-filled face.

He placed a tender kiss at the corner of her mouth. "Wrap your legs around me, Summer."

He jerked in pleasure when silky thighs tightened around his hips. "That's it." He kissed the other corner of her mouth. He withdrew and slowly sheathed himself back into Summer's heat. "Don't hold back, love. It takes two to get where we're going."

Summer loosened her grip on the bedspread and hesitantly reached for him.

Beads of sweat broke out across his brow and a smile brightened his flushed face. "That's it, love."

She met his next thrust and buried a soft cry of pleasure against his throat. She reached for his searching mouth as he increased the pace. Tongues plunged and sweetly curled around each other. Feverish hands caressed and explored as the tempo and sensations spiraled out of control.

"Eben!" Summer cried out as the safe, secure feeling dropped out from underneath her and she was left soaring, with Eben as her only anchor.

Eben felt her contractions close around him and plunged one last time. His arms tightened into a steel band around her while he called her name over and over.

Seven

Summer heard a rough moan, and it gently shook her into a blissful half-woken state. A wistful smile brushed her lips as she ran a slender foot up a coarse-haired calf. She nestled closer and lightly caressed a smooth, firm hip.

Eben groaned and placed his throbbing arousal in her grasp.

Awareness flooded Summer's dream-filled senses. She quickly released him and jerked into a sitting position. She grabbed the sheets, yanked them up to her neck, and squinted into the darkness. "Eben?"

Not knowing if he should be amused or annoyed, he asked, "Who did you think you were teasing?"

"Teasing?" Oh, Lord, her dream had been reality.

He had been awakened by the feel of Summer's inquisitive fingers on his chest. After four minutes of untold torture he had finally reached his limits and had shown her the fruits of her labor. "What would you call trailing hot little fingers down my chest, around my belly button, and up my thigh?"

"Forward" and "promiscuous" crossed her mind as embarrassment flooded her face. It was true: she had fondled, caressed, and awakened the poor man in the middle of the night. Her breasts pleaded for his touch, and the tingling between her thighs attested to her need. She had surfaced from the most erotic dream of her life, to find out it was real.

Eben cursed the darkness. "Summer?"

"I'm sorry."

He reached for the lamp next to the bed. Light flooded the room, causing both occupants of the bed to blink and shield their eyes. Eben adjusted first and stared at Summer's red face. "What are you sorry for?" he asked.

"Waking you."

"Waking me, or touching me?"

Summer's face burned even more as she looked everywhere but at Eben. "Waking you," she answered honestly.

Bewildered, he ran a hand through his sleep-tousled hair. She was doing it again, holding back. Why? She hadn't been an innocent virgin, and he knew she had enjoyed what they had shared earlier. "Do you like touching me, Summer?"

Her fingers trembled slightly as they clutched the sheet tighter. "Yes."

Eben breathed a sigh of relief. With slow, gentle pressure he lowered her hands and the sheet to bare her breasts. He studied her expression as with a finger he drew a heated path from the corner of her mouth, down her throat, and over the creamy mounds. Excitement and pleasure flushed her cheeks. "Do you like it when I touch you?"

Her nipple pebbled into hardness under his touch. She nodded her head and whispered, "Yes."

A moist kiss showered the nipple with appreciation. "Then I don't see a problem, do you?"

Summer sank her fingers into his hair and raised his mouth up to hers. Her softly whispered "No" was lost in the rustling of sheets as she lay back down and pulled his weight with her.

Summer tugged the sheet over her head and cursed the brilliant morning sun. Whose bright idea was it to do the entire eastern wall in windows? She lowered the sheet and peeked at the pillow next to hers. It was empty.

With a groan she buried her head under the pillow. The previous night, not only had she learned to take the first hesitant steps, she had walked, run, and galloped right into her first vacation fling. And with the wrong man! She and Eben had absolutely nothing in common. Well, she did like to run her fingers over his chest, and he had seemed to like that. Then there was that neat little trick he could do with his tongue.

Heat swept up her cheeks. Heaven help her! Little Summer Hudson from West Bend, Iowa, was having lustful thoughts about a CPA. A tall, dark, and handsome CPA who made common sense desert her and her blood boil, but a CPA nevertheless. What else could they have in common besides great sex?

Cautiously she sat up and squinted into the room. Where was all the light coming from? Her glance followed a dazzling beam of sunlight up to the ceiling. She stared at two large skylights and shook her head. Was Eben insane? Who could possibly sleep in all this glaring cheerfulness?

The room was tastefully done in wood and various shades of blues. It was a man's room, with only a small gathering of towering plants clustered in a corner to break the simplicity. A frown pulled at her mouth as she spotted her dress hung up and hooked to the closet door. Her shawl was neatly draped across the back of a chair that held a tidy pile of her undergarments. Either Eben had been busy, or he had a band of servants hiding around here some place.

Her gaze flew to the bathroom door as it opened. Summer's glance slid down Eben's chest to the thick blue bath towel draped low on his hips. Why had no one ever told her how sexy a man could look wearing only a towel and a smile? The appeal of tight blue jeans and brief swimsuits was legendary. It took a really homely male not to get his money's worth out of a tuxedo. But terry cloth was highly underrated.

"Good morning, sleepyhead," Eben greeted.

She tried to run her fingers through her curls as she glanced at the clock. Quarter after seven on a Saturday morning, and he was acting as though it were noon. "Morning," she answered, her voice low and rough.

Eben turned and walked toward a bureau where he pulled out some clothes. "There's coffee downstairs."

He definitely had servants. She sat enthralled as the towel hit the floor and Eben pulled on clothes.

He finished tucking his T-shirt into his shorts and

picked up the damp towel. "Why don't you take a shower while I cook some breakfast?"

"Breakfast?"

"Saturday's specialty is French toast."

Summer's stomach growled. "That's the best offer I've had all day."

Eben opened his mouth to voice another offer, but quickly closed it. He walked to the bed and placed a light kiss on the end of her nose. "Hurry up or I won't sprinkle powdered sugar on yours." He dropped the towel in the bathroom hamper and headed out the door.

Summer scrambled off the bed, grabbed her clothes, and dashed into the bathroom. A look of horror struck her face as she stared into the mirror. Curls sprang in every direction and makeup was smeared under her eyes, giving her the appearance of a demented raccoon. Thankful that Eben was gentleman enough not to scream in terror, she turned on the shower.

Fifteen minutes later she opened the door and muttered a dark comment at the sunlight drenching the bathroom through the skylight. Maybe Eben was suffering from a deadly disease that only overexposure to the sun could cure.

She slipped on her dress and frowned at the neatly made bed. Curious, she walked over and lifted the spread. Crisp blue-and-white plaid sheets had replaced the solid blue ones from the previous night. She glanced around the room to make sure a maid wasn't hovering nearby. Suppressing the desire to leave a tip, she followed her nose toward the ravishing scent rising from the kitchen.

Several minutes later, Summer pushed away her

plate and groaned. "That was delicious. Where did you learn to cook like that?"

"Pure survival. I like to eat." He stood up and started to gather the empty plates.

She finished her coffee and placed the empty cup in the dishwasher. "It certainly beats cold pizza any day." She nervously ran her hands down the flaring skirt of her dress. Considering this was her first breakfast with him, she did all right. "Well, I guess I'll be going."

Eben lost his grip on the syrup bottle and banged his knee on the open door of the dishwasher. "You can't go."

"Why?"

He rubbed the red welt on his knee and closed the door. "I just thought that after last night . . ." He grimaced as her chin rose an inch. "I mean . . ." He shoved his fingers into his hair. "Dammit, Summer. I want to spend some time with you." A smile lurked in the depths of her blue eyes. "I would like to get to know you better."

"Better than last night?" Her voice held awe.

Eben chuckled and pulled her into his arms. "You just stop me when you've had enough." He kissed her nose as it tilted up in the air. "That is not what I meant. I thought we could pack a picnic lunch and take the boat out."

"On the lake?"

He chuckled again. "Where else would we go?" Knowing her fascination with the legendary Champ, he dangled the bait. "Up past South Hero there are dozens of isolated coves."

Excitement gleamed in her eyes. "On the New York or Vermont side of the lake?"

"Vermont."

She glanced down at her dress. "Do I have time to change and grab my camera?"

"Help me pack the basket and I'll personally escort you back to your cabin. I wouldn't want to lose you." Eben lowered his mouth to taste the morning sweetness of her lips.

Summer's arms encircled his neck as he deepened the kiss. The embers of passion kindled and flared. A soft protest tumbled off her lips as he broke the kiss. Her eyes shone with anticipation. "How could you possibly think you'd lose me after that?"

Eben's eyes turned serious as he searched her face. "Eben?"

He shook his head slightly. Crazy thoughts were rustling in his mind again. "Come on, sleepyhead. If we don't leave soon, we won't get there till dark."

Summer took another look at Eben's hat and burst out laughing. Shiny silver and brass lures and brightly colored feathers connected to a multitude of hooks dangled from every available inch. "The reason you're not catching anything is your hat is scaring all the fish away."

Eben tried to maintain a straight face as he glared across the boat at Summer. "Your nose is going to peel if you don't put something on it."

With a smile she dug into her tote bag and pulled out a bottle of sunblock. "Touchy about the hat, are we?"

"I'll have you know my mother bought it for my birthday."

"Boy, what did you ever do to her?"

Eben chuckled and reached for a bottle of apple juice. "Besides ruining her golden years by not presenting her a grandchild to bounce on her knee?"

"Ah, one of those." She stopped rubbing the white lotion on her nose and replaced the bottle in the bag.

Eben's eyes narrowed at the tone in Summer's voice. Curious, he asked, "What did your parents buy for your last birthday?"

Summer stared out across the isolated cove. "Blue-chip stocks."

Eben frowned. What kind of parents gave their daughter stock for a present? Adjectives like "practical," "rich," and "unimaginative" came to mind. Injecting lightness into his voice, he repeated her question. "What did you ever do to them?"

She forced a weak laugh. "Besides being born, choosing the wrong career, and not marrying the right man?"

He pounced on the most important part. "Right man for whom, you or them?"

Summer smiled for the first time since the conversation had turned serious. "For them."

"Want to talk about him?"

"No, it's not only boring, but ancient history." She glanced at her legs and reached for the tote bag again.

Eben was mesmerized by the long, smooth strokes she used to apply the tropical-smelling lotion. "What career did your parents pick out for you?"

"Nuclear physics."

Astonishment held him speechless for a moment. "And I thought my parents' choice was bad."

"What did your parents pick out for you?"

"Brain surgeon."

Summer whistled. "Why didn't you become one."

With a sheepish smile he admitted, "I faint at the sight of blood."

Compassion and understanding swelled in her heart. They had a common bond. Both had gone against their parents' wishes. "What did they do when you told them you wanted to be an accountant?"

"Dad bought me a calculator, and my mom gave me the ugliest tie I have ever seen. What did your parents do?"

"Threatened not to pay my tuition."

Eben frowned and reeled in his line. Uncharacteristically, he made an assumption about people he had never met. He didn't like Summer's parents. "What do your parents do?"

"Dad teaches chemistry at a university, and Mom's a biochemist for a privately funded research lab."

"Impressive."

Summer glanced over at Eben. "Is it lunchtime yet?"

Eben cringed at the sudden change of subject, but he followed her lead. "Sure. There's a little deserted island about two miles from here. How about if we wade ashore and have a picnic?"

"A real deserted island?" she asked, intrigued.

He secured his fishing pole and hat under the seat. "Yeah, and it's large enough to hold two trees and our blanket."

He stood behind the wheel and drove the boat. When they neared the island, Summer grinned. "I thought you said there were trees?"

Eben dropped anchor. "They're baby trees." He

helped Summer out and handed her the picnic basket.

"They're bushes, Eben," she said, spreading the blanket. "They'll never grow up to be trees." She took out sandwiches and tried to make room on the blanket for Eben. If there were nine square feet of land on his deserted island, she'd eat the wicker basket. She pulled her legs up and rested her chin on her knees. "Come here often?"

"First time." He bit into his sandwich and mumbled, "I was saving it for a special occasion."

Summer raised her hand and waved to a water-skier, who was fifty yards away. "Nice and private too."

Eben grabbed her slender ankle and pulled, forcing her to fall against him. "Privacy wasn't the intention."

"What was?"

He brushed a bread crumb off her lower lip. "Time and space to get to know you better."

"And are you?"

"Every minute I'm with you I find myself falling deeper under your spell."

"What spell?"

"You have bewitched me since the first night I saw you walking past my house along the shore."

Summer gazed into his serious brown eyes. "My common sense told me to stay far away from you."

"Don't you listen to your common sense?"

Her hands lightly caressed his chest through his T-shirt. "If I did, I would have married Richard."

His fingertips skimmed her thighs. "Why didn't you?"

"We would have driven each other crazy." Her palms

itched to run over his broad shoulders. "He was a perfect male who wanted a perfect wife."

He toyed with the hem of her shorts. "So?"

"I'm not perfect."

Eben chuckled, cupped her hip, and pulled her closer. "No one is, Summer."

"Some are closer than others."

He recalled the time she had called him perfect. He arced his hips and pressed his arousal against her. "If I were perfect, Summer, I would be able to control this."

Awareness and need flared in her eyes. "If you were perfect, you would have chosen a more private island for lunch."

Eben bent and captured her lower lip between his teeth. The gentle thrust of Summer's hips caused him to groan and release her mouth. "Do you know what my definition of perfect is?"

Summer closed her eyes and savored the kisses he was trailing down her neck. "What?"

Fire was blazing in his eyes when he looked up into her face. "Being inside you. Feeling you around me." His fingers shook slightly as he traced the delicate shape of her jaw. "Perfect is when you don't hold back and love me with everything you have."

Tears pooled in her eyes and her voice quivered when she said, "You don't mind?"

Bewildered, he asked, "Mind what, darling?"

"Me touching you."

Understanding dawned. With the little he knew about her parents, they didn't seem like an affectionate pair. And if they approved of Richard the perfect, he could safely lump him in the same category. He uttered a curse as another boat whizzed by. "Come on, we're leaving."

"Where are we going?"

He started throwing half-eaten sandwiches back into the basket. "My house, your cabin, or anywhere we won't be interrupted." He dumped out their drinks and threw the empty bottles in with the lunch. "I'm going to show you exactly what your touch does to me."

Summer got to her feet, half-anxious, half-leery, and whispered, "Oh."

A sweet, satisfied smile curved Summer's mouth as her breathing slowed to a nearly normal rate. She raised her head and glanced around the room. Her voice held wonder as she gazed down at the man lying satiated under her. "We didn't even make it out of the kitchen."

Eben chuckled. "Be thankful we made it into the house." He pressed a light kiss on her swollen lips. "Now do you believe me when I tell you that your touch inflames me?"

She brushed a lock of damp hair off his forehead. "Is it my touch, or were you always this excitable?"

He reached up and cupped both her cheeks. "Do I look like a man who habitually makes love on my kitchen floor?"

She rubbed her cheek against his palm. Tops, shorts, and sneakers were scattered over the once-immaculate room. Her cream-colored lace bra was dangling off the leg of an overturned chair, and a pair of white jockey shorts decorated the countertop. She wiggled her hips and smiled at his instant response. "CPAs aren't allowed to make love in kitchens?"

"It's not the kitchen, it's the floor." He groaned as his desire rekindled. Why couldn't he get enough of her? "Do you have any idea how hard it is?"

Summer felt the stirring of his arousal against her and grinned. "I'm beginning to."

"Not that, the floor." He forced his lips into a pout. "I think I may have skinned several parts of my body."

She ran her tongue over his cute pout. "I think you're getting soft in your old age."

Eben thrust his hips.

"Then again, I could be mistaken." Summer chuckled. "How about we go upstairs and wash off the suntan lotion that's now all over us?"

Eben helped her to her feet, wrapped an arm around her shoulder, and hustled her from the room. "Maybe you should look me over. My injuries might be fatal."

Summer's laughter filled the house. "Eben James, you certainly aren't like any accountant we have back in Iowa."

"Eben, I think the steaks are burning."

He lifted his lips from the enticing spot behind her ear and glanced at the grill. "You could be right." He flipped the steaks and frowned at the crisp meat. "Mind a little charcoal with your dinner?"

Summer looked at the steaks and smiled. If he thought these were burnt, what would he think of her barbecue attempts? "They look great. I'll go finish setting the table."

She walked into the kitchen and from the refrigerator pulled the salad she had made earlier. The delicious aroma of buttermilk biscuits rose from the stove, and two baked potatoes were sizzling away in the microwave. Lord, all they needed was a turkey and it could be Thanksgiving.

She was setting the last bowl on the table when Eben joined her. "It looks and smells delicious."

"Thanks, but it was a joint effort. Let's eat before it gets any later."

Eben helped himself to the salad. "Planning on going somewhere?" he asked jokingly.

She cut open her potato and smeared butter on it. "I was hoping to make it to the cove tonight." She held her breath and waited for his reaction. They had avoided the subject of Champ, even though they both knew that that day's boat trip had been for her benefit.

His teeth crunched a carrot slice as he studied her. Why would a beautiful, intelligent woman believe in a sea monster? A little voice inside his head gave a sudden kick. If it wasn't for Champ and the two separate sightings by the cove, Summer wouldn't even be here. "I have a thermos around here someplace. We could fill it with coffee."

Summer looked up as a radiant smile lit her face. "Thanks."

Eben felt his toes melt. He'd spend the rest of his life in a rubber dinghy just to keep seeing that smile.

"Do you feel it?" Summer whispered.

The hair on the back of his neck stood on end, and his fingers tightened on the flashlight as he glanced from the shore out across the lake. Unearthly silence

surrounded them, and he could see nothing unusual. So why did he feel he could step out of the raft
and into another dimension? He shook his head and
watched the ducks clustered around the shore. The
three mallards, who had been waddling happily moments before, turned to the lake and stood perfectly
still. The group of boisterous ducks that had been
swimming had suddenly become quiet. "It's a phenomenon."

Summer glanced at Eben. Was he actually admit-
ting to feeling the strange pull of twilight? "Yes, it is.
Twice a day it's neither day nor night."

He zipped his jacket and shivered as the shroud of
darkness started to descend. "Twilight."

Summer lowered her binoculars. "You should experience twilight when the light wins over the darkness."

"Eerier?"

She sighed. "Breathtaking."

Eben smiled at the picture she made huddled in
one of his old sweatshirts. Yes, she was breathtaking.
"I would like to witness that phenomenon with you
one day."

"It's a date."

"Summer, have you seen my black belt?"

She pulled a baggy sweatshirt over her head and
jammed her feet into shoes. "No, what does it look
like?"

Eben ran a hand down his jaw and groaned. He
had forgotten to shave. "It's long and black. I can't go
to the office looking like this. Can you look for it
while I shave?"

Summer started to dig through his closet. "You should organize your time better."

He halted at the bathroom door and stared at her. "Me! Who's idea was it to go sea-serpent hunting at dawn?"

With a triumphant cry she pulled a black belt off a hook. "You were the one who insisted on coming along." She handed him the belt.

"That's a jeans belt. I'm looking for my dress belt."

Summer studied the belt. A jeans belt—what in the hell was that? "Well, whose idea was it to make love when we got back?"

Eben smiled and placed a kiss on her surprised lips. "I am a genius at times." He playfully swatted her rear and disappeared into the bathroom.

Her laughter filled the room. Lord, she couldn't get any happier, except maybe if she could find the right belt.

Five minutes later she admitted defeat as Eben buttoned up his shirt. "Sorry. All I could find were three brown belts, one gray, and one that looks navy blue."

Eben picked up the gray one from the pile she'd made on the bed. "This one will be fine, Summer." He kissed her. "Don't look so depressed."

"I could cook you some breakfast."

A quick glance at his watch had him jamming his feet into a pair of shoes. "Sorry, love, I'm running late as it is."

A brilliant smile lit up her face as she hurried from the room. "I know!"

Eben yanked a tie out of the closet and headed for a mirror. Three minutes later he was running down the steps. "Summer?"

She met him at the bottom of the stairs and walked with him to the door. She handed him the half-filled thermos from that morning and a hot Pop Tart wrapped in a paper towel. "Breakfast is the most important meal of the day, you know."

He looked dubiously at the sugar-coated pastry. "You remember where I told you the spare key was?"

"Don't worry, Eben. I'll lock up when I leave."

"I was more concerned with you being here when I get home."

"About five-thirty, right?"

He pulled her close and kissed her with heated passion. When desire started to spiral out of control, he broke the kiss and shuddered. "Woman, I'm going to miss you."

In ecstasy, she opened the door and grinned. "I'll be here when you return."

Eight

"Aurora Dove, are you sure?" Summer asked.

"Tea leaves might fudge a little, but they never lie."

Summer gazed down at the brown remains in the cup. They had just predicted the ruin of her life. "It was only going to be a fling. This wasn't supposed to have happened."

Aurora Dove stood up and dumped the mushy leaves down the drain. "Come on, Summer, you had to realize it was happening."

Every time he touched me, I knew, she thought. But she said, "We don't even live in the same time zone."

"A simple inconvenience, not an impossibility." Aurora Dove set a plate of cookies on the table and placed the teakettle back on to boil. "Why did you allow me to read the leaves if you already knew?"

A sheepish smile curved Summer's mouth. "I was half hoping you'd tell me it was indigestion and it would go away."

"The moon's not full, and indigestion doesn't last an entire weekend." Aurora Dove answered. "I'm afraid to tell you this, Summer, but you're in love."

"This definitely wasn't on the agenda for my vacation," she muttered, with a dejected sigh. "Great, I get to take a broken heart back to Iowa for a souvenir."

Aurora Dove placed a cup of steaming tea in front of Summer. "It's a real shame about the youth of today."

"What?"

"Back in the sixties we knew how to fight for what we wanted. We fought for the end of a war, for equal rights, and for freedom. Today's youth gives up too easily. If it isn't handed to them on a silver platter, they have no idea how to get it."

Summer's eyes narrowed as she stared at the woman who she'd thought was a friend. "I have fought for every single thing that I have ever wanted in life."

Playing the devil's advocate, Aurora Dove countered with "Then you must not want Eben."

"Of course I do. Who am I supposed to fight? There's no other woman, or anyone else to confront."

"Ah, but there is."

"Who?"

"You are your own worst enemy."

Incredulous, Summer cried, "Me?"

"I don't see anyone else sitting here talking to an aged flower child when she should be home planning to fight for her future."

"This is the nineties, Aurora Dove. We don't believe in fighting."

Aurora Dove smiled slyly. "I don't mean putting up

your dukes. There are better ways to a man's heart."

"Through his stomach," Summer finished the cliché.

Aurora Dove's laughter filled the kitchen. "What I was referring to is a little bit lower."

Summer fought a blush and reached for a cookie. "You're terrible. How does Franklin put up with you?"

A saucy grin curved Aurora Dove's lips. "I know the way to his heart."

Summer's laughter joined Aurora Dove's as Franklin stepped into the kitchen. He placed a light kiss on his wife's nose. "Hello, Summer. Haven't seen you around for a couple of days." He glanced at the two giggling women. "What's so funny?"

"We're planning the downfall of one of your comrades, darling," Aurora Dove purred.

Franklin trembled. "Lord help him. Anyone I know?" His gaze jerked to Summer. "Eben?"

"We weren't planning anything," Summer said defensively.

Franklin's eyebrows rose, and he stared pointedly at his wife. "Don't put any crazy ideas into Summer's head." A look of concentration crossed his face as he grabbed a cookie off the plate. "Aurora Dove?"

"Yes, dear."

"Use logic with Eben. Cooking, organization, and fishing are your best chances," he said. "The boy needs a good shaking up. He's been set in his ways too long. Give me a yell, Summer, if you need any help," he threw over his shoulder as he walked out.

Summer frowned when Aurora Dove gleefully rubbed her hands together. "Forget it! I'm not planning anything."

Aurora Dove pouted and took a sip of tea. "Are you

at least going to wow him with a culinary feast tonight?"

Misery washed over her. "On a scale of one to ten, my cooking rates a two."

"It can't be that bad."

"I sent him off to work this morning with cold coffee and a Pop Tart."

Aurora Dove smartly turned a laugh into a cough. "What about organization?"

"If my checkbook's within a hundred dollars of what my bank statement says, I'm happy."

"Fishing?" Aurora Dove asked hopefully.

Summer glared across the table and went back to sulking. She might as well pack up the car and head back to Iowa.

"You could always use my original idea. I know some pretty interesting tricks, thanks to Sammy and company."

"Who is Sammy?"

"Houston. Samuel Houston. It's amazing what you can pick up if you were a soiled dove in a past life. Maybe we should hypnotize you and see what you did in your past lives?"

"I won't use sex to hold any man's attention, let alone one I'm in love with." Annoyed, Summer stood up.

Holding back a grin, Aurora Dove asked, "What are you going to do?"

"What I should have done as soon as I knew—tell him!" She stomped to the door.

Aurora Dove saluted her with a cookie. "Excellent plan. It's straightforward and courageous, totally brilliant. He won't even realize what hit him."

Exasperated, Summer snapped, "Go pick dandelions, or whatever it is you use in your tea," and walked out the door.

Aurora Dove burst into a gale of laughter. They were perfect for each other. Not a flicker of doubt crossed her mind. She was going to be seeing Summer for years to come.

Eben took off his glasses and rubbed the bridge of his nose. It was no use; he couldn't concentrate. He glared at the stack of files containing quarterly returns. Whose bright idea was it to become an accountant? If he had chosen to teach instead, he would still be home with Summer. With an impatient curse he reached for the phone and punched in his home number for the fifth time.

Where was Summer? Why wouldn't she pick up? he wanted to know. The receiver was slammed back into the cradle when only his answering machine answered. This was ridiculous. He couldn't work. When he added up two plus two, he got four, which reminded him of the four seasons, and summer was a season.

His secretary, Martha, had been frantic by the time he showed up fifteen minutes late for work. Relief turned to concern as she stared at the half-eaten Pop Tart in his hand and the silly grin spread across his face. The third time he had caught her staring, he straightened his ill-matched tie and grinned. He had heard the words ". . . as a hatter" before Martha went into a coughing fit and claimed something was tickling her throat.

Frustration laced through his body as he pushed back his chair and stood up. He jammed several folders into his briefcase, turned off the light, and walked out of his office. "Martha?"

Worried eyes peered over the top of silver-framed glasses. "Yes, Eben?"

"Stop what you are doing and lock up. I'm giving you the rest of the day off."

Martha glanced at her watch and gasped. "It's only two-thirty."

"I know how to tell time, Martha."

Concerned, she asked, "Aren't you feeling well?"

Eben frowned. Was he such a bad boss that a few hours off caused his secretary to become flustered? "I'm fine. I just can't allow you to continue working when I'm knocking off early."

Martha's fingers trembled as she fidgeted with a pencil. "Is everything all right at home?"

"It's fine, Martha." He perched a hip on her desk and leaned closer. "When was the last time I gave you a raise?"

The pencil went flying out of her hands and bounced off a file cabinet. "The first of January, sir."

Eben concentrated and stared at the woman who had been his right arm for the past eight years. Each January, like clockwork, he'd called her into his office and offered her the customary cost-of-living increase in salary. "How would you like a 5 percent increase, effective immediately?"

Huge gray eyes blinked. "It's only July!"

"I know. Isn't it wonderful?" Eben leaned forward and placed a kiss on a motherly cheek. "You're invaluable to me, Martha. It's the least I can do. Thank you."

Bemused, she watched as Eben stood up and headed toward the door. "Eben?"

"Yes?"

"All this because it's July?"

"No," he opened the door. "But Summer had something to do with it."

Martha's mouth fell open. She had gotten a 5 percent raise just because it was summertime. Well, huckleberries and crab cakes, what had happened to the past eight years' worth of summer raises?

Eben shifted the flowers and briefcase to his other hand as he tried to jiggle the key into the lock. The door swung open, and he stepped into his hall. "Summer!"

No answer. He walked into the living room, noticed magazines scattered across the coffee table, and called her name again. Silence. He placed the bouquet of yellow roses in a vase, glanced around the other rooms, and headed upstairs.

The master bedroom was empty. What did he expect? He was home over two hours early. He peeled off his tie and hung up his suit. His white shirt found the hamper, and his shoes were wiped clean and replaced in the shoe rack. After a quick shower, he changed into a pair of gray cotton twill pants and a lighter gray shirt. He hung the belts that were still piled on the bed back into the closet and neatly made the bed.

He was about to leave the room when he walked over to the window and glanced at the beach. A smile of relief brightened his expression. Summer was sitting on the end of the dock. With hurried footsteps he went to join her.

Summer heard Eben's steps as he walked down the

dock. Panic increased the tempo of her heartbeat and caused her hands to tremble. He was home early, leaving her no time to figure out a way to fix it.

Eben sat down next to her. "Hello, sunshine."

Summer kept her eyes cast down and studied the slow swing of her bare feet above the water. "Hello, Eben. You're home early."

Something was wrong. He could feel it down to his toes. This was not the greeting he had been hoping for. "Summer?"

She didn't lift her face. "Yes."

He cupped her chin and forced her to look at him. His heart contracted with fear when he saw the anguished look on her face. "What happened?"

"You're going to be mad."

Eben looked around to see what was different. She was in one piece, his house was still standing, and his boat was peacefully bobbing on the lake. "You're scaring me, Summer. Tell me what happened."

Her voice quivered. "I think I broke it."

"What?"

Summer pointed in the direction of a dilapidated old rowboat pulled up on the shore.

"You broke Franklin's rowboat?"

"No, what's in it." She bent her head and went back to staring at her feet.

Eben slowly got to his feet, walked down the dock and over to the rowboat. Emotions flared and quieted as he looked down. There lying across the broken middle seat was his Shimano ST 2000 reel and Crossfire rod. Fifty yards of six-pound-test line were wrapped around the seat, over the reel, under his tackle box, and through the oarlocks. Good Lord, what had she done?

He gingerly picked up the rod. It rose two feet in the air before being stopped by the tangled fishing line. He pulled a knife from the tackle box and cut the line.

"Sorry."

Eben, startled by Summer's sudden appearance at his side, turned and mustered a smile. "Can I ask what you were doing?"

"Fishing."

Horrified, he forgot his concern over his reel as he looked at the rickety rowboat. "In that thing?" he cried.

"The boat was the easy part. It only leaks a little."

A shudder slid down his spine. She could have been killed. Franklin's rowboat, christened the *Titanic*, was the disgrace of Pine Harbor. The year-rounders had been known to pile into their cars and speed to the shore just to watch naive tourists take the boat out. Wagers were placed on the outcome of the junket. If the tourist looked strong and intelligent enough to start bailing as soon as the *Titanic* took on water, wagers were low. But if the visitor's seafaring experience was limited to tug boat races in the bathtub, money flashed fast and furious on whether the visitor would make it back in time. "Did Franklin know you borrowed that boat?"

"No, why should he? Aurora Dove was with me."

Eben ran his fingers through his hair. "I should have guessed. I was hoping you possessed more common sense than to take that boat out!"

"Why are you shouting at me because of the boat? Aren't you supposed to be ranting and raving about your fishing pole?"

"I can fix the reel. What I couldn't fix is you drowning or getting seriously hurt."

A small smile tilted the corner of her mouth. He wasn't furious that she had made spaghetti out of his string, but he was concerned about her. "We didn't go out far, and Aurora Dove did help bail."

Eben's lips twitched at the vision of Aurora Dove bailing. "One last question—why did you go fishing? Saturday you didn't show any signs of being interested in the sport."

Summer shuffled her feet on the pebble-strewn beach. She couldn't just blurt out that she was in love with him. Somehow, killing a trout with torturous hooks to prove your love didn't seem romantic. Settling for the partial truth, she said, "You seem to enjoy it, and I like the lake and fresh air, so I wanted to try it."

"Why didn't you ask me to show you instead of Aurora Dove? You couldn't have picked a worse instructor. The woman doesn't eat meat or fish. What would she know about fishing?"

"Apparently not much," Summer muttered. After storming out of Aurora Dove's house, she had started to feel guilty. She was, after all, the one who had gone over there. It wasn't Aurora Dove's fault that their outlook on the subject of love differed. By lunchtime she had picked a small bouquet of wildflowers and offered them to Aurora Dove as a peace offering. Half an hour later Summer found herself drifting in a leaky rowboat, cursing whoever invented fishing and Aurora Dove's distorted sense of humor. They had just pulled the seeping tub up on the beach when they heard Eben's car. With a smile Aurora Dove excused herself and discreetly disappeared into the surrounding trees, leaving Summer alone to explain the water-logged boat and ruined equipment.

Eben chuckled at Summer's disgusted expression. His mood lightened with the fact that she was trying to learn to fish to please him. It didn't matter that she had jammed, tangled, and scratched his favorite and most expensive reel. The same reel he used to snag the Pine Harbor Day fishing championship in June with the prize catch of a thirteen-pound-six-ounce trout. She had cared enough to try.

With a tender smile he pulled her into his arms. "Since I seem to have a couple of free hours, how about we take *my* boat out and I'll give you a lesson?"

Summer bit her lower lip and looked at the reel still clutched in his hand. "Can you fix it?"

"I have a couple of other poles in the garage we can use for now. I'll look at this one later," he said, setting it down.

A beautiful smile appeared on her lips as she pressed in closer. "I missed you today."

Eben groaned and kissed her with heated passion. Desire rocked her senses as his tongue swept over her lips and into her mouth.

Before he could lose control, he broke the kiss with a sharp intake of breath. "What are you doing to me? I can't work, I gave my secretary a raise, and I broke the speed limit driving home to you." He kissed her brilliant smile until a moan of need rose in her throat. His teeth playfully and tenderly nipped at her ear. "You don't really want to go fishing right now, do you?"

Summer pressed her hips against his straining arousal. "That's awfully interesting bait you're using."

Eben gave a shout of joy and swept her up into his

arms. His eyes darkened with hunger as he carried her the distance to his bed.

Eben stepped over a pile of books and riffled through a stack of magazines. "Summer, have you seen a folder marked 'Henson'?"

She marked the page of the book she was reading with a candy wrapper. "No, what does it look like?"

"A folder. Brown, letter-size, with 'Henson' written in black magic marker on the tab." Exasperated, he dug through the magazines again.

Summer frowned as she joined in the search. For the past three days Eben had become upset and frustrated over the simplest things. She knew he was working long hours against the quarterly tax return deadline. "It's not out here, Eben. It must be in your office somewhere."

Eben glared at the pile of magazines. How could one person have such a variety of interests? The magazines ranged from wildlife, scuba diving, and agriculture to an Ellery Queen mystery magazine. He glanced at the cover of the book she had just put down—a biography of a Civil War general. How could he possibly keep up with them all? "It's not in my office. It has to be buried in this mess somewhere."

"Mess?" She thought she had been meticulous about keeping all her stuff together.

"Look at it. You can't possibly enjoy reading it all."

"You're right. Some of it is boring and trivial."

"Then why do you read it?" he asked.

"I'm a teacher. My students expect answers to every question they ask." Hurt that he didn't understand, she asked, "How do you think teachers stay so smart?"

"You read all this to keep current?" His arms swept through the air to encompass all the literature scattered about.

"A mind's a terrible thing to waste."

Eben sat down on the couch, rested his elbows on his knees, and closed his eyes. She clasped her hands together and quietly sat next to him. Puzzled and hurt by his behavior, she asked, "Would you rather I returned to my cabin?"

His head snapped up. "No!" Fear shot through him at the thought of her leaving. "I didn't understand."

"Understand what?"

"Why you never complained."

Summer looked from Eben to the magazines. "Complained about what?"

"For the past three evenings, after dinner, I have disappeared into my office for hours. Most women I know would find that highly objectionable, but not you. You sit out here night after night being content to read enough stuff to make an owl go blind."

"What did you expect me to do when you worked? You explained the corporate tax deadline to me. I don't have a problem with it."

Exasperated, Eben snapped. "I do!" He hated the infringement on his time. He hated working in the other room while Summer was cuddled up on his couch with a book. He wanted to take her for a moonlight cruise on the lake, dance till dawn, or spend a week snuggled in bed with her.

Summer blinked in astonishment. "But you love your job."

"I did—before you waltzed into my life and turned it

upside down." He reached for her and tugged her into his arms. "I hate the IRS and its quarterly returns for keeping me away from you."

Her fingers played with the buttons on his shirt. "It's only for a little while longer." Three buttons parted, and Summer pressed little kisses down the middle of his chest. A satisfied smile curved her mouth when the thundering of his heartbeat echoed against her lips. Lord, how she loved this man. "You can last that long, can't you?"

Eben leaned back, dragging her with him. "No" was uttered against the slender column of her neck.

Summer shifted into a more comfortable position. "It could be worse."

Desire pounded in his groin as his hands caressed her thighs. "How?"

She slowly rocked her hips and smiled invitingly down at his flushed expression. "It could be April."

Eben's reply was lost when she claimed his mouth.

The soft tinkling of the bell above the door greeted Eben as he walked into Bass Heaven, Plattsburgh's finest fishing-tackle shop. He strolled down the center aisle, under the hundreds of rods forming a striped canopy, and headed for the rear of the store. He spotted a familiar bald head bent over a huge magnifying glass. The man was deftly tying a miniature feather around a fishing hook. Fascinated, Eben quietly stood and watched as Gus expertly cut the thread. How anyone had the patience to tie their own flies was beyond him, but Gus was the master in Plattsburgh.

Aged gray eyes looked up from the finished hook and smiled. "Eben!"

"Hello, Gus. I see you've been keeping busy."

Gus gestured to the opening in the countertop. "Come back here and cast your eyes on this beauty."

Eben made his way behind the counter, around stacks of cartons, and stepped over an open tackle box. "Some day, Gus, you are going to break a leg back here. Don't you ever clean up?"

A harsh chuckle wheezed from Gus's throat. "Jumping Jehoshaphat, if I put everything away, I won't be able to find anything."

A soft whistle of appreciation flitted through Eben's pursed lips as he studied the fly under the magnifying glass. "Large mouth bass in Clingman's Cove."

Gus gave another chuckle. "Only you could have guessed that in one try."

Concerned, Eben glanced up. "You're not going out, are you?" Two years ago, Gus had been diagnosed with a chronic lung problem. Standing in hip waders for hours in the early morning mist was forbidden.

"And risk the wrath of Myrtle? Are you crazy, boy? That woman is bound and determined to keep me around to her dying day just so she can have someone to criticize."

Eben grinned and shook his head. "How is Myrtle?" The woman was equivalent to a saint in his mind. Any woman who had put up with Gus for the past fifty years, borne nine children, and had forty-seven grandchildren and over a hundred great-grandchildren deserved to be nominated to sainthood.

"Full of opinions. Just ask her anything, she has an opinion on it."

Not wanting to get involved in family matters, Eben looked back down at the fly. "Who did you make it for?"

Gus's eyes narrowed. "That depends."

"On what?"

"Who's offering me the most greenbacks."

Eben bit the inside of his cheek to prevent a smile from showing. His voice was emotionless as he named a fair price.

"Well, son, looks like you're going to have bass for dinner." Gus reached under the counter for a small clear plastic box. He unclasped the fly and tenderly placed it in the box. "Is that all you came in for?"

Eben frowned and handed Gus the brown paper bag he had been holding. "I need your help. They say you're the best at fixing any reel, so I brought this to you."

Gus's white eyebrows rose as he took the bag and dumped the contents on the counter. "Lordy, boy, that's your ST 2000! What happened to it?" He picked it up and carried it over to the magnifying glass. A disgusted sigh left his cracked lips. "Don't tell me, let me guess. You let a woman use it."

Eben shuffled his feet and tried to bury the desire to apologize. It had nothing to do with Summer being a woman; it had to do with her being an amateur fisherman, or was it fisherperson? "It was an accident. Do you think you can fix it?"

After several more minutes of poking and pulling at the line, Gus looked up. "It might take a few days, but I think so." With a shrewd gaze, he studied Eben's expression. "It must be love."

"What?" Eben croaked.

"Only love would cause a man not to commit murder when his best reel has been so blatantly violated. If the female in question is still breathing, let alone in the same state, it's true love."

Eben snapped his mouth closed. Gus was right. He was in love with Summer! It wasn't uncontrollable lust he had been feeling, it was uncontrollable love. He was in love with a schoolteacher from Iowa who believed in sea monsters. How in the hell had that happened?

He ran a trembling hand through his hair and looked around. He had to get out of there to think. He needed fresh air. With jerky movements he started to leave. "I'll pick it up in a couple of days, Gus. Thanks."

Gus's eyes gleamed with laughter as he watched Eben hurry past the bobbers and sinkers and out the front door. He carefully picked up the plastic box with the fly nestling in the bottom and chuckled. Eben had it bad, he thought. The poor boy. Women! Ugh. They were the blight of all good fishermen.

Nine

Eben jammed his hands inside his pants pockets as he stared at the painting. The artist had captured each and every one of his feelings and applied it to a canvas. The night that he first saw the painting with Summer, he had been impressed. Now, standing in the bright light of the unrelenting sun, he was awed.

His life had been like the dark lake, with him content to stay behind the swirling fog. Summer was the lightening of the sky, the heat that burned away the morning mist. He and the painting had something in common—they were both standing in twilight.

The artist had portrayed lightness conquering darkness. Would his life be brightened by Summer's love? Would darkness prevail when she left? What if she didn't love him? She had never said the words, but at times a flicker of something special shone in her eyes. His heart lifted in hope. She might not love him but, but she would, or his name wasn't Eben Elliott James.

A confident smile teased the corner of his mouth as he walked into the art gallery.

Summer carefully lowered her camera and binoculars to the coffee table, then frowned at the muddy footsteps she had trailed across Eben's living room. She had wiped her sneakers until the squishing of the gunk between her toes forced her to stop. She needed a shower. Hell, she needed to be run through a car wash five or six times. She would have gone to her cabin to clean herself up, but all her clothes were in Eben's closet.

Careful not to touch anything, she tiptoed up the stairs. A cry of distress filled the bathroom as she glanced at herself in the mirror. She was worse than what the grateful farmer, who had brought her home in the back of his pickup truck, had said. Mud and dirt streaked her face and hair. With a disgusted sigh she reached up and pulled a piece of green slime from a golden curl and flung it into the sink.

That was absolutely the last time she would help some dumb animal. She pulled her damp, filthy T-shirt over her head, glanced at the white hamper, and pitched it into the sink. Her soggy bra followed. When she had set out this morning in her car, she had been clean, full of enthusiasm, and clutching a detailed map of twelve miles of uninhabited shoreline. She unsnapped her shorts and yanked them down her dirt-smeared legs. A shudder slid down her spine as something squished in her once-white sneakers. What had she ever done to deserve this?

Six miles from her cabin she had spied a calf stuck knee-deep in a mud hole, and her heart had softened for the poor baby. Its pitiful bleats tore at her soul. Carefully placing her camera and binoculars safely out of the way, she had waded in after the lost animal. Fifteen long minutes later she began to understand how a mud turtle must feel. The calf obviously didn't comprehend what needed to be done. Every time Summer got too close to its face, a huge, moist pink tongue licked her. She had picked herself up out of the mud for the fifth time when the calf's owners showed up. The farmer was considerate enough not to show his amusement; his teenage son wasn't. A blush had swept up her grubby cheeks as the farmer, wearing knee-high black boots, calmly walked through the mud and picked up the calf.

Her shorts and panties landed on the white-tiled floor as she stepped into the tub. Summer turned on the faucet, sat on the edge, and held her sneaker-clad feet under the running water. At least the farmer had been kind enough to send his smirking son and the ungrateful calf walking back to the pasture before offering her a ride home. Common courtesy had made her insist on riding in the back. She'd get Eben to drive her back to her car later tonight.

She untied her sneakers and slipped them off. "Yuck!" She shuddered as brown goop oozed out and slithered down the drain. She held the sneakers under the running water until it ran clear, and then she tossed them at the other end of the tub. Setting the adjustments on the faucets, she closed the shower curtain and stood under the warm spray.

Ten minutes later Summer stepped over her muddy shorts and reached for another clean towel.

She wrapped her hair turban-style and tucked another towel around her breasts. Ignoring the filthy shirt in the sink, she opened the medicine cabinet and borrowed Eben's razor.

Eben frowned as he spotted pieces of straw littering his driveway. He carried the painting in one arm and lugged his stuffed briefcase with the other. By next quarter he was going to have extra help in doing the mounds of tax forms. The paperwork that was crammed into his briefcase was the last he was tackling alone. When these forms were completed, he was dedicating every available second to Summer and winning her love. He had come home from work early to surprise Summer, only to find she wasn't home.

His face contorted with disgust when his hand grabbed the muddy doorknob. What in the hell was going on? he wondered. He quietly entered his unlocked house and placed the painting and briefcase against the hall wall. His eyes widened with alarm as they followed a trail of grimy footprints through the hall and up the stairs. On silent feet he cautiously climbed the steps. A frown pulled at his mouth as he entered the master bedroom—it was empty. Bewildered, he followed the fading trail to the closed bathroom door. He put his ear to the door and listened to the sound of water being run in the tub. Burglars don't take baths in their victims' homes, he told himself. Or do they? With slow steady movements he twisted the knob and flung open the door.

The sudden slamming of the door against the wall caused Summer's hand to jerk, and she cut herself with the razor. Surprised and in pain, she cried, "Eben!" as a burning sensation attacked her ankle.

"Summer?"

"Who did you think would be in the bathroom?" She grabbed a washcloth and wet it before applying it to the cut. Blood had already dripped into the tub.

"My God, what happened?"

Summer jerked around at the strange tone in his voice. Concern for Eben overshadowed the burning in her leg. His face was deathly pale. Good Lord, he looked as though he were going to pass out at the sight of blood! "Don't look at it." She jumped up from the side of the tub, and pushed him onto the closed seat of the commode. "Put your head between your knees."

Eben shook his head and tried to chase away the black spot before his eyes. "I'll be fine in a minute. I have to get you to a hospital."

"What for?" she asked.

Eben tried to rise, felt the room tilt, and quickly sat back down. "You were in a car accident! A doctor has to look at you."

Summer bit her lip. Eben was suffering hallucinations from lack of oxygen to his brain. Was that common with fainting? Lord, she never actually saw anyone faint before, but wasn't he supposed to turn goofy after he hit his head? She sat down on the side of the tub and asked, "Why do you think I was in a car accident?"

Eben gulped in air. "Your car is missing, you trail mud, dirt, and straw through the house, and you're bleeding to death in the bathroom." The faint rushing sound left his ears. "Did you run off the road into some farmer's field?"

"I didn't have an accident, Eben."

His gaze took in her wrapped hair and the enticing view of cleavage above the white bath towel around her body. She looked as though she'd just stepped from a bath, all squeaky clean and sexy as hell. He glimpsed the white washcloth, which was slowly turning pink, wrapped around her ankle. "What happened?"

Summer stared at the third button on his shirt while she explained.

After she was through, Eben slowly stood up, stepped over the muddy shorts lying on the floor, and squatted down in front of her. He reached behind her to shut off the spigot and saw his razor in the tub. "And you cut yourself shaving?" He picked up the razor and carefully set it on the side. He seemed to be trying hard not to comment on her stupid rescue mission.

"It's just a nick."

He raised a doubtful brow, but didn't look. "I startled you when I burst in here like a deranged idiot, didn't I?"

Summer looked down at the three-inch gash. "It's just about stopped bleeding. Legs are such tricky suckers. One little nick and wham! Saint Valentine's Day Massacre all over again."

Eben placed a finger under her chin and forced it up. "I'm sorry."

"For what?"

"Causing you pain. I followed the footprints thinking it was a burglar."

"In the bathroom?"

His thumb gently caressed her lower lip. "I guess living with you takes some getting used to."

This was the first time he had mentioned her living there. She had come home with him several nights before and had never gone back to her cabin, except to pick up clothes and some books. He had even helped her pack up all her junk food and had carried the box to his house. Her gaze locked with his. "I guess it does."

Eben's fingers trembled as they slipped around the back of her neck. "I was going to wait for a more romantic moment, but I can't. I love you, Summer."

Summer gazed at his handsome face. It didn't matter that he didn't believe in Champ, that he had graduated from the school that said "Show me he's real," while she had graduated head of the class at the "Show me he isn't real" school. What did it matter? He loved her.

Happiness and the promise of forever gleamed in the depths of her shining blue eyes. "This *is* the most romantic moment of my life." She felt the gentle pressure of Eben's fingers and closed the distance between them. Her mouth softened under his demanding kiss. With a gentle purr she swept her tongue over his lower lip.

Eben broke the kiss and held her shoulders. "Well?"

Summer blinked. Then a soft smile touched her lips as she tenderly cupped his warm cheeks. "I love you, Eben."

Moisture gathered in his eyes as he swallowed a sudden lump in his throat. His voice was husky with emotion as he choked out the word "Good" before picking her up and carrying her out of the room.

•   •   •

"Summer, why is there a snowman in the hall?"

She dropped the book on cryptozoology, dashed into the hall, and threw herself into Eben's arms. She got the greatest feeling in the world when he walked through the door each evening. Well, the second greatest feeling. Her beaming face looked up at him. "Isn't he wonderful? While I was in Wilsboro this morning I found this charming shop that specializes in Christmas."

Eben kissed her inviting mouth. "It's only July."

"It will be August next week, so Christmas is right around the corner."

He glanced at the four-foot-high papier-mâché snowman and chuckled. "Let me guess. Christmas is your favorite holiday."

"How did you know?"

"Old Frosty here, the ornaments crowding the bookshelves in your cabin, and the collection of corn husk angels on top of my stereo gave me the hint." He placed his briefcase on the floor and walked with Summer to the kitchen. "What were you doing in Wilsboro?"

She watched as he pulled a package of frozen chicken out of the freezer. "I was talking to a lady who spotted Champ two years ago." She took the chicken out of his hand, shoved it back into the freezer, and pulled out a couple of hamburger patties. "You don't mind if we have something fast tonight, do you?"

"Why?"

"You've been promising to go out with me to the

cove, but we always manage to be otherwise occupied during twilight."

Eben wiggled his eyebrows and grinned. "Are you complaining?"

"Not about that, but I really would like to go out to the cove tonight." She noticed his frown. "You don't have to come. I can manage by myself."

His frown turned into a scowl. "Of course I'm coming with you. I don't like it when you go out alone."

"Are you coming to be with me, or because you think I'll fall overboard and drown?"

Eben looked at her serious expression and sighed. He knew they weren't discussing her being capable of handling a raft; they were talking about Champ. For days he had purposely maneuvered her into being otherwise occupied during her favorite spotting time. He wanted her to forget about Champ, to forget about returning to Iowa. He needed her with him, and he didn't intend to share her with a phantom creature. But for tonight he would give in.

His gentle kiss softened her expression. "Loving you gives me the privilege to worry, but I will go with you tonight because I want to be with you."

He didn't say another word for the next hour. He was unusually silent throughout dinner and their walk along the beach later, even as they paddled in her raft to the cove.

Summer lowered her binoculars as darkness obscured her view. A chill swept through her body as she glanced over at Eben. Was he regretting her constant presence? Did men need their space? Lord, why hadn't he ever talked about their future? In three weeks she'd be heading back to Iowa if something wasn't said soon.

But everything had to work out. When two people loved each other, surely no problems were insurmountable. And she was sure Eben loved her as much as she loved him. Otherwise he wouldn't respond to her simplest touch the way he did.

As a matter of fact, Eben encouraged and cherished her displays of affection, which were tentative at first. When she was a small child, her parents had been embarrassed by any show of affection. There were never kisses to make it better, only lectures on acting like a proper lady. Richard had reinforced the lessons taught throughout her childhood. He had insisted on no public display of affection, no hand holding, no stolen kisses, and a respectable distance between them on the dance floor. She was at all times to act the lady his position at the bank deemed his fiancée should be. Within a month she knew their engagement was a dreadful mistake. What she thought was love had been an attempt to gain her parents' approval. And her show of independence had gained her father's indifference and her mother's rage for letting the most eligible bachelor in West Bend get away.

With Eben physical contact was as natural as breathing. He taught her there was nothing shameful in expressing their love, and she was every inch a lady in his eyes.

Everything between them just had to work out. But looking at him now, she felt a shiver of apprehension. He seemed so far away from her at that moment, even though they were in a tiny raft.

Eben stared at the darkened waters and ran theconversation through in his mind one last time. *"Mom, Dad, I would like you to meet your future daughter-in-law, Summer Hudson. She's a school-teacher from Iowa who chases sea monsters. After the kids are born, we're going to have them tested for previous lives and Aurora Dove is going to read their dominoes."*

Eben dumped the remaining coffee in his cup into the lake. It was no use; he couldn't see himself saying that. Summer never came out and said she believed in past lives, just that she didn't discount them. Well, hell, wasn't that the same thing? Her obsession with Christmas he could live with; it was his favorite holiday too. The fact she was a schoolteacher was fine with him. If she wanted to continue her career, even after the children came, she'd have 100 percent of his support. It was the sea monster bit that had him worried. If she believed in Champ that year, what would she think up next year? Would she pack up the kids and fly to Ireland to look for leprechauns? Or take up mountain climbing in Tibet to hunt for the abominable snowman? He didn't even know if she wanted children.

She was a puzzle. She was sweet, gentle, and surprisingly innocent. Her views, even when they opposed his, were always logical, and she usually had facts and figures to back her up. So why would she spend an entire summer vacation searching for a nonexistent sea serpent?

"Eben?"

He came out of his musing at the sound of her voice. "I'm sorry, did you say something?"

"I asked if you're ready to leave."

Eben glanced around. The night had descended

without his consciously being aware of it. "Sure. Are you finished?"

Summer picked up an oar and started to paddle. Her voice held a touch of sadness. "Yeah, I think I'm finished."

Eben ran a frantic hand through his hair and glanced down the shoreline. Where was she? He had been home from work for over two hours, and still no Summer. No notes, no messages on his answering machine, nothing! He glanced in the opposite direction and cursed. He headed through the woods toward her cabin.

Eben glared at the deserted cabin. Where in the hell could she be? She was always at his house when he came home. She was the reason he hurried through his day, pouring ten hours' worth of work into eight. He needed her. What if something had happened to her and she needed him? He didn't know where to find her.

Sweat broke out across his brow as he jogged to Franklin and Aurora Dove's house. Maybe they would know where she was.

"I'm sure you're worried over nothing, Eben," Aurora Dove told him, glancing at the clock. "It's not even eight o'clock. Summer probably got involved with something and lost track of time. I do it all the time."

Eben paced the length of their kitchen. "She's always at the house when I come home."

"Is her care there?" Franklin asked.

"No."

Franklin's voice was hesitant as he continued. "Are her clothes and belongings still at your place?"

Eben paled. He never checked!

He ran out, and Aurora Dove and Franklin exchanged curious glances as the screen door slammed behind Eben.

Summer jumped from her car and hurried to the house. She opened the door and wildly waved a piece of paper. "Eben!" She raised her voice and shouted again. "Eben, guess what I got!" She skidded into the living room and spotted Eben sitting in the gathering dusk. "Eben?"

He didn't take his eyes off her as he slowly rose to his feet. "Are you hurt?"

A shiver went through her at his emotionless voice. "No."

"Were you in an accident?"

Summer's feet halted halfway across the room. "No, I'm sorry I'm late, but wait till you see what I have."

She was safe and unhurt. He'd endured three hours of pure hell and all she said was "I'm sorry." His voice rose like thunder as he made a fist and roared, "Where in the hell have you been?"

Summer stepped back.

"Do you have any idea of what I've been going through? I checked your cabin, hiked to the cove, and made a fool out of myself in front of Franklin and Aurora Dove."

Summer took another step backward as Eben advanced. Where was her sweet, even-tempered lover? Who was this bellowing maniac?

The fear gleaming in her eyes didn't register through the fog swirling in Eben's frightened mind. He'd thought he had lost her, and all she could do was stand there. "Why didn't you call?"

Summer flinched at his tone and backed into a wall. Her voice was low and wavering as she answered with the truth. "I lost track of time."

Eben groaned as he jammed his fists into his pockets. "You lost three damn hours?" he shouted.

Tears pooled in her eyes. "I said I was sorry."

"And that's supposed to make it all right?" He noticed the tears and tried to lower his voice and remain calm. He hadn't meant to frighten her. "Where were you?"

"Port Henry."

His hands unclenched and he relaxed. There was going to be a logical explanation. With a slight smile of encouragement he waited for her to continue.

Summer relaxed at his smile. He wasn't mad any longer. When she'd traveled to Port Henry, she'd thought she was on a wild goose chase, but then the golden egg had been handed to her. "Yesterday while I was in Wilsboro, I picked up on a rumor of a woman who took a picture of Champ two weeks ago."

Eben tensed. "What?"

"I knew you would be excited," Summer said, grinning. "Her name is Ilene Pennyworth, and she's a retired physician. Her hobby is bird-watching. Can you believe that? A bird-watcher snaps the shot that makes a legend into reality." Summer held up an excellent reproduction of the photograph. "See, she even gave me a copy."

Eben glanced at the black and white copy and grimaced.

"You should have heard the stories Ilene told me about Champ. In the past two weeks she has gathered more information than I have all summer." Excitement shimmered in her voice. "She has maps, charts, and copies of the Lake Champlain Phenomenon Investigation reports. It was incredible, Eben, you should have been there."

His control snapped. She had put him through the worst three hours of his life for the rambling of some old woman and a fake photograph. "There are no such things as sea monsters!" he yelled.

Summer's mouth fell open in astonishment.

"Ilene Pennyworry belongs in a padded cell, and that is obviously a fake picture!"

Summer straightened to her full height of five feet five inches. "It's Pennyworth, and the picture is genuine."

"Did she try to sell you a bridge too?"

Frustration and anger caused her voice to rise. "That was a cheap shot. You'll have to eat those words when the photo is proved genuine."

"Ahhh. What did she do? Send it to Disneyland for verification?"

"No, the Smithsonian Institute is running a densitometer study and enhancement on the original print and negative before the print is released to the press."

She was using logic again. And logic couldn't explain away the three hours of sheer terror she had just put him through. He folded his arms across his chest and scowled. "From now on you are not to go looking for imaginary sea serpents."

Flabbergasted, Summer cried, "What did you say?"

"You heard me. I won't have you risking your neck on something that's not there."

"It's my neck!"

"Not while it's under my roof!" he yelled.

Dead silence filled the room.

Eben jammed his hands back into his pockets and stared up at the ceiling. He wanted to recall those words but couldn't—he had meant them. If she stopped this lunacy about Champ, everything would work out, but if she continued this folly, he'd lose his mind. He couldn't concentrate at work for fear she was out on the lake alone and something might happen to her. When he had returned from work that night, all of his worse fears had materialized and bombarded him until he had become this raving maniac standing before her. He couldn't go on.

Summer glanced at the floor and willed the tears not to fall. Her anger had turned to despair at his ultimatum. He was telling her that she could share a questionable future with him only if she obeyed his rules. Eben was looking for something she wasn't—the perfect woman. Her voice was weak with unshed tears. "I'll go gather my things." Her head was held high as she walked out of the room.

Ten

Eben finished his morning coffee without taking his eyes off the painting. It wasn't fair. The artist's twilight was conquered by dawn, while darkness prevailed over his own personal twilight. Summer was gone.

The previous night he had stayed in the living room mutely staring out at the lake while Summer had made six trips to her car. A piece of his heart had splintered off and died with each closing of the front door. His head had cried out for him to help Summer carry the boxes; his heart had refused to turn around and watch her leave. His heart had won. After the door had closed for the sixth time, he had heard the faint sound of her car starting and driving away. She hadn't even said good-bye.

Hours later he had pulled the painting out of the hall closet where he had hidden it. He had planned on giving it to Summer on the day she agreed to become his wife. With the painting in one arm and a bottle of Canadian whiskey in the other, he had headed for his office to toast twilight.

He glanced at his watch. He was going to be late for work and he didn't care. What in hell did it matter if he figured out a way to save a client some hard-earned tax dollars? Twilight would occur again, but Summer wouldn't be there to share it with him.

"You look like hell."

"Thank you, Aurora Dove, for that friendly update," Summer snapped. She shoved a pile of magazines off the couch and onto the floor. "If you don't ask any stupid questions, you may have a seat."

Aurora Dove shuddered as Summer ripped open a package of chocolate cupcakes. "Is that your dinner?"

"No, I picked up a hamburger." She left out the part about ditching the greasy burger after one bite. Summer held out the cupcakes. "Do you want one?"

Aurora Dove shook her head, walked over to the kitchen table, and glanced through the scattered maps and papers. Her hand reached out and picked up the photocopy of Ilene Pennyworth's picture. "Is that Champ?"

Summer cursed at the pain on her sunburnt nose. "Don't be an idiot, there are no such things as sea monsters. That's a figment of an old woman's imagination."

Aurora Dove chuckled. "Imagine that, photographs of a person's imagination. What will they think of next?"

Summer glanced over her shoulder and mustered her first smile of the day. "Technology. They can put a man on the moon, create life in a test tube, and make bombers invisible, but they can't find one shy, elusive twenty-foot sea monster in a lake."

"Priorities, Summer, priorities. We need invisible bombers so we can drop more bombs and kill more people. We can't feed all the children in the world, but let's make some new ones. Space exploration .is semibeneficial. The way I figure it, if we keep on destroying this planet, we are going to need another one real soon."

"That's it, Aurora Dove, cheer me up."

Aurora Dove smiled and walked over to the refrigerator. "How did you get so burnt anyway!"

"I climbed up that 'little hill' Ilene Pennyworth was at when she spotted Champ. I stayed there all day and didn't see a thing. Except birds."

Aurora Dove cracked an ice tray and dumped the cubes into a clean dish towel. "Here, put this on your face."

Summer glanced at the towel. "Why?"

"Your face looks like the hind end of a lobster." Aurora Dove handed her the ice pack. "The ice will draw the heat out. I have something for the pain at home." She walked toward the door. "Make sure the ice covers your eyes too. It will help with the swelling. So you won't look like you've been crying."

Summer glared at the closed door. Some people had the nerve. She sucked in a breath as she placed the cold pack on her face. She was listening to Aurora Dove only because she was nice enough not to have mentioned Eben.

Five minutes later Aurora Dove returned, and despite Summer's protest, she smeared juice from a long sliced-open leaf on Summer's face.

Summer tried to frown. Her face was frozen solid and she wasn't sure if her mouth turned down. "What is that stuff?"

"Aloe. The Indians used it for burns."

"I'm not an Indian."

"I'm sure the plant doesn't know that." She finished the job and asked, "Where was your hat?"

Sitting on top of Eben's refrigerator. "I must have misplaced it."

"Why didn't you use sunblock, then?"

Because it was in Eben's bathroom. "I forgot. If you drop the lecture, I promise to be more careful tomorrow."

Aurora Dove handed Summer a plate of bran flake biscuits and oatmeal cookies. "Try eating something nutritious and going to bed. You look beat."

Summer covered up a yawn. "I do eat nutritious stuff."

Aurora Dove raised an eyebrow. "I've seen the inside of your refrigerator. Would you like to restate that?"

"I do eat nutritious stuff when I go shopping."

"Better, Summer, but not convincing." Aurora Dove opened the door. "Keep that face out of the sunlight tomorrow or you'll scare Champ into extinction when he does decide to show his handsome profile."

Eben pushed the wrinkled green peas around with his fork. Two nights without Summer and he had reverted right back to disgusting frozen dinners. After he had come home from work, he had sat in the living room for hours waiting for Summer to walk by on her way to the cove. She never came. She hadn't gone that morning either, or the morning and evening before. Maybe she had given up on Champ. Or maybe she had gone back to Iowa. No, he knew she was still around, or Aurora Dove would have told him. He'd asked the older woman to check on Summer for him.

He left the table and dumped the uneaten dinner into the garbage. He had spent the entire day worrying about her. When he had added up the same column of figures for the third time and come up with three different answers, he knew he had lost. Love couldn't be rolled into one nice little package.

With tired footsteps Eben walked out onto his deck and down the stairs to the edge of the lake. He picked up a handful of pebbles and made them skip across the calm surface. Between each throw he turned in the direction of Summer's cabin and thoughtfully stared at the woods.

Several minutes later he returned to his house. He entered the kitchen and saw a pair of high-heeled shoes under the table. Every time he turned around, he found more of Summer's possessions. He walked past the refrigerator, refusing to look at the straw hat perched on top, and headed for his office. He had work to do, considering he wasn't getting any work done in town.

Half an hour later, Eben twirled the glass in his hand and listened to the sound of ice cubes sloshing in the whiskey. His briefcase lay unopened on top of the desk, and the dust cover wasn't even removed from his adding machine. He picked up a paperweight, turned it upside down, and gently lowered it to its original position. Snowflakes danced through the water, a blizzard falling on the miniature town trapped in the plastic bubble. Summer had bought him the paperweight a week before. She had delighted him with the two-dollar gift, while he had reached the limit on his gold credit card with the painting he never had a chance to give her. He turned the paperweight again. What a pair they made.

His hand was reaching for the bottle to pour a second drink when the doorbell sounded. He jumped up and hurried to answer it. His hopeful expression fell when he opened the door to Aurora Dove. "Oh, it's you."

"If I wasn't so concerned, I'd let you stew longer," she said, marching past him into the living room.

He frowned and closed the door. "What's wrong?"

"Have you seen Summer?"

Eben's face drained of color. "What?"

Aurora Dove patted his arm. "Now don't get excited, Eben."

"You lost her!"

"I did not. You asked me to check on her, not tail her. I just thought you ought to know that she's not in her cabin."

"When was the last time you saw her?"

"Last night around six."

Eben looked out the glass doors toward the lake. It was pitch dark out. "Was she okay?"

"She was grouchy, sunburnt, and suffering from indigestion, but otherwise she was fine." Aurora Dove wrinkled her nose at the empty candy wrappers and cups littering the coffee table. "I went to see her around six, but she wasn't home. So I waited until it was dark. When she still didn't show up, I started hoping she'd be here."

"Did you notice if she packed up?"

"Her stuff is still there, but her car's gone."

Eben released the breath he'd been holding. He reached for a jacket and flashlight. "Come on, let's start back at the cabin."

Aurora Dove silently followed Eben through the pines and up on to Summer's dark porch.

He shone the light through her living room window and jerked in surprise when a smiling snowman grinned back. "Do you have any idea where she might have gone or what time she left?"

"No, but she has maps marked and dated."

Eben spun around and pinned Aurora Dove with the light. "Where?"

Aurora Dove held up a key ring. "On the kitchen table." She inserted a master key into the lock. "This goes against my principles on privacy, but Summer should have been home hours ago."

Eben pushed open the door even before the key was removed, and hurried to the table. Aurora Dove turned on the light and grabbed the map she had seen the previous night. "See, she has areas highlighted and dated."

He snatched the map out of her hand and quickly scanned it. His breath hissed out between his teeth when he located the dates for that day and the one before. Summer was twenty-five miles from home and in the most desolate stretch of shoreline on the entire lake. A thunderous curse filled the cabin as he dashed for the door. "Aurora Dove, if I'm not back in three hours with Summer, notify the police."

Summer directed a venomous remark against the great blue heron as she stumbled backward and landed for what seemed like the hundredth time in the rapidly cooling water of the lake. She pushed a soggy curl out of her eyes and glared at the nasty bird. "You stupid yellow-eyed fiend, I'm trying to help you. Stop trying to bite me."

She shivered and glanced at the frightened animal in the pale moonlight. Strength, pride, and doom gleamed in its eyes. It was the doom that had kept Summer diligently working for the past several hours.

She had stayed at her post longer than she had intended. When the evening sun had started to set she had known she had to go. Hiking through the underbrush in the dark with only a small flashlight wasn't her idea of fun. She had just finished packing her gear when she had been startled by a great blue heron swooping down. In the approaching dusk it resembled a pterodactyl. Fascinated, she had watched as it stalked the shore and silently waded through the shallow water at the lake's edge. She had been yanking on her backpack when the heron started to flap its wings and struggle wildly. Getting as close to the lake as possible without startling the heron, she had raised her binoculars. A tangled mess of fishing line was wrapped around the heron's long, stiltlike legs. For half an hour she had watched the heron try valiantly to free itself. Then she had dumped the contents of her backpack on the ground, looking for anything that would cut fishing line, and had come up empty-handed. With a silent prayer for divine guidance she had slowly waded into the lake and hoped that a bird would be easier to rescue than a calf.

Eben parked his car behind Summer's and quickly got out. She had to be around here someplace. He turned on his high-voltage flashlight and followed the path she must have taken through the brush. His hands were shaking as he crested the hill.

He heard a distant voice and swiftly swung his light in its direction. The beam faintly illuminated Summer and a blue heron standing in about nine inches of water. Relief washed over him. He cupped his mouth and yelled, "Summer?"

Summer turned her head. Lord, she was never so glad to see another person. Her heart pounded in relief when she heard Eben's voice. He had come looking for her! "Down here, Eben."

He quickly descended the faint path. He stopped at the edge of the lake, shone the light on her scattered gear, then turned to her. "Are you all right?"

"Fine. Do you have a knife on you?"

He glanced at the bird standing four feet away from Summer and sighed. The tangled mess of fishing line told the story. "I see you're still into rescuing animals."

Summer bit her lower lip. "I couldn't leave him."

Eben noticed the exhaustion etched into Summer's face, the drenched clothes and hair, and the sadness in her eyes. "I know you couldn't." He pulled a small penknife from the pocket of his jeans and took a step toward the bird.

"Don't!" Summer cried out. Eben went perfectly still. "He doesn't understand we're trying to help. Every time I get close, he tries to bite."

Eben glanced back at her. "Did he get you?"

"Only a couple of halfhearted nips. I think if he was really trying, I'd be sort some fingers already."

Eben surveyed the four-foot heron. "Okay, buddy, we do this the hard way." He walked to Summer and handed her the light and knife. "You distract Grouchy here, while I sneak around behind him. I'm going to try to straddle him so he can't use his wings, and I'll do my best to keep his bill away from you. Your job is going to be cutting away the line as fast as you can." He took off his jacket and threw it over by the empty backpack and picked up a large rock. He slowly walked back toward the bird and lowered the rock six feet away. "Hand me the light." He positioned the light on the rock, so it was shining on the bird. "Now we at least have both hands free." He glanced over at Summer and smiled. "Ready?"

"Try not to hurt him, please."

Eben frowned. "I'll fight fair if he does."

Summer took a deep breath. "Here goes." She started to walk around one way while Eben circled the other way. When she had the heron's undivided attention she faked a move toward him.

Eben leaped and tried to lock the heron's wings to its body with his knees. His right hand closed around its long bill, while his left hand tried to steady the heron.

Summer ducked beneath a wildly flapping wing and started to slice through yards of fishing line. Eben cursed as an enormous wet wing slapped against his face. His sneakers started to slip against the rocky bottom. "Hurry up, Summer."

Summer dodged the wing and stifled a cry as the heron kicked with its almost free leg. "Hold him still. I don't want to cut him."

Eben yelled a warning as the heron jerked back its head and cracked him in the groin. He fell backward into the water, still grappling with the struggling bird.

"Be gentle with him, Eben." She was sitting in the water, trying to keep the bird's feet still, and slashing at the nylon line. "I'm almost done."

Eben sucked in air between his teeth. He was ruined for life! He would never have children to bounce on his knee. His muscles were straining against the savage strength of the heron.

"Done!" Summer yelled. She looked at the wrestling pair and snapped, "Eben, stop playing and let him go."

Eben released his hold. The heron quickly stood and, without stopping to say thanks, gracefully flew away. Eben glared after the winged demon and was about to mutter an opinion on roast heron when Summer turned shimmering eyes on him and said, "Thank you, Eben."

His chest puffed slightly as he graciously helped her to her feet. "You're welcome, but it was nothing."

Summer gathered the scattered pieces of fishing line and handed Eben his penknife. "How did you know where to find me?"

"Aurora Dove became worried when you didn't come home by dark."

She glanced down to hide the hurt in her eyes. *Aurora Dove was worried, but not you.*

"We broke into your cabin and found the map where you mark your daily trips." He gazed at her bent head and fought the urge to pull her into his arms. "Let's get out of the water before you catch cold." He picked up the flashlight and lit the way.

Summer walked to the edge of the lake and started to jam things back into her pack. "Thanks for checking up on me. I was running out of ideas on how to free the heron."

Eben grimaced as water tickled his toes. He hated wet sneakers. "I'm sure you would have managed." Was this what they had come to? Making polite small talk. Didn't she miss him, as he missed her? He draped his jacket over her shoulders and picked up her backpack. "Come on, let's get you home, you look dead on your feet."

She hastily wiped a tear, then led the way back to their cars. It wasn't her fault he found her looking like an extra from *Night of the Living Dead*. He was the reason she couldn't sleep or eat properly. She stopped at her car and handed him his damp jacket. "Thanks again, Eben."

He opened the door and tossed the pack onto the passenger seat. He wanted to wrap her in his warmth and tell her everything was going to be okay. He wanted to kiss her until she melted against him and promised to come home with him. He ran his fingers through his damp hair. "Summer?"

She heard the low tremor in his husky voice, and her insides dissolved. In a breathless voice, she whispered, "Yes?"

His gaze locked on her lower lip. He couldn't go through another night like that night. He wanted her safe, and she wanted legends. "Drive carefully."

As she climbed in behind the wheel, she blinked back the tears that came once more and started the journey back to her cabin. With every mile and every glimpse of his headlights in the rearview mirror, her heart grew heavier. When she pulled into the campground, she waved to Franklin and Aurora Dove, who were sitting on their porch, but didn't stop. She didn't want to talk to anyone tonight. All she wanted was a hot shower, a soft bed, and Eben's love.

Eben stopped his car in front of Franklin's house and lowered his forehead to the steering wheel. Summer was safely back home—no, she was safely back at her cabin. But she belonged in his bed that night, and every night for the rest of her life. His hands hadn't stopped trembling yet, his groin throbbed with discomfort, and his heart ached for Summer.

"I see you found her," a female voice remarked.

He glanced up at Aurora Dove and Franklin. "She was rescuing a blue heron who was trapped in fishing line."

"Always knew she had a heart as big as New York," Aurora Dove said with a chuckle. "Is the heron okay?"

Eben gave a brief description of how they had saved the ungrateful demon. When he finished, he was amazed he was actually laughing along with Franklin and Aurora Dove. It hadn't seemed funny at the time. He said good night to Aurora Dove as she dashed into the house to check on a batch of biscuits.

"Franklin, why would an intelligent, sane woman spend her days chasing after a yellow-polka-dotted, fire-breathing sea monster?"

Franklin frowned at his friend. "Is that what you think Champ looks like?"

"What else would a sea monster look like?"

"Didn't you ask Summer?"

"No, we never discussed Champ."

Surprised, Franklin asked, "Why?"

"Because every time we did, we ended up arguing." Eben glanced down the dark road that led to Summer's cabin. "She's risking her neck chasing after a legend."

"I've never seen Summer risk her neck. She seems like a very practical woman to me."

"She goes out alone in the raft."

Franklin chuckled. "You go out alone fishing in your boat all the time."

"That's different," Eben snapped.

Franklin crossed his arms and smiled. "How?"

Eben opened his mouth to comment and then closed it shut. Why was he asking Franklin's advice? He was married to the strangest woman on the New York side of the lake. "I'm going to catch pneumonia if I don't get out of these wet clothes. Tell Aurora Dove thanks again." He backed up the car. "See you around, Franklin."

The older man raised an arm in farewell. His voice cracked with laughter as he said, "Pleasant dreams."

Eleven

Summer smiled at the teenage girl behind the counter. "Double scoop of Chocolate Almond Delight, please."

After getting her ice cream, she paid the girl and walked out onto the crowded sidewalk. Crafter's Alley was doing a booming business. She found an empty bench, stretched her legs out into the sun, and ran her tongue around the rapidly melting confection. From behind huge sunglasses she watched as hordes of humanity waltzed by. Children were begging for treats, teenage boys tried to act cool, and lovers held hands. Everywhere she looked, she saw people enjoying their vacations.

Yesterday she had spent the day walking along deserted shores spending more time exploring her emotions than the lake. When Eben had shown up in time to rescue the heron two nights earlier, she had known that the love she felt for him wasn't going to go away. It was deeply embedded in her heart. She wanted to wake up next to her *perfect* man for the rest of her life.

Summer glanced as a young mother wetted a napkin and wiped the chocolate ice cream off her two-year-old son's face. Her heart contracted as the mother lovingly kissed the clean cheek, reached for his small hand, and walked away. That was how a mother was supposed to express her love, not by belittling the child for being sloppy.

Her whole life had been spent trying to please a mother who was insatiable. Summer's grades had never been good enough. The year she made straight A's, her mother had demanded to know why she wasn't the captain of the high school's debating team. When she'd told her mother that her prom date had already been accepted into Columbia's prelaw program, her mother had informed her that only Harvard men amounted to anything.

Now Summer laughed and drew curious looks from passersby. She grinned back at a five-year-old girl who was staring at her as if she were crazy. After eight years she finally saw the absurdity of it—her own father never even went to Harvard. It wouldn't have mattered if she had followed her parents' wishes and gone into nuclear physics, she still wouldn't have been good enough for them.

Summer finished her cone and used her napkin to wipe a splotch of ice cream on her shorts. She had three weeks left of her vacation and she was going to do exactly what she wanted. She walked past the families and giggling girls and headed to the edge of the lake, away from the crowd.

She found a solitary rock and sat. A sad smile touched her mouth as she stared out onto the lake.

Sorry, Champ, you're going to have to pose for someone else. As of today I'm out of the monster-investigating business. It didn't matter that she hadn't captured the legend on film for all the world to see. She had discovered something more significant on Lake Champlain—love. Her top priority was Eben. She wasn't ready to walk away from the best thing that had ever happened in her life.

Her steps were light as she retraced her trail back to Crafter's Alley. Her smile was dazzling as she walked into a small shop and marched up to the counter.

When the young man glanced up from his pad, he was momentarily stunned by the beautiful woman standing before him. "May I help you?"

"One large pizza with the works, to go."

Summer pulled in front of her cabin and picked up the still-warm pizza from the passenger seat. Eben was due home from work soon. She would need this first decent meal in days to fortify herself for the battle of her life. She was reaching for the cabin key when a car pulled up behind hers. Curiously she watched as Eben's secretary, Martha, stepped out from behind the wheel. "Martha?" What was she doing here?

The older woman nervously glanced around and fidgeted with the purse clutched in her hand. She looked at the pizza box Summer was holding. "I didn't mean to disturb your dinner."

"Come on in, Martha." She opened the cabin door. "Did you have dinner yet? There's plenty here."

Martha stepped into the cabin and hid a smile. It

was just as she had pictured it. She had met Summer twice when Summer had stopped in the office to visit Eben. Both times had reinforced her opinion of the woman who had stolen her boss's heart. Summer was the complete opposite of Eben. "One little piece would be nice, if you're sure there's enough."

Summer swept papers and maps off the kitchen table and onto the couch. She placed the pizza in the center and went to rummage up two clean glasses. There was only one reason why Martha was here, and that was Eben. Martha could have the entire pizza if she had any information that would help her win back his love. "Sit down, Martha. Is diet cola okay?"

"Fine." Martha sat.

Summer passed Martha the first slice of pizza. "So what brings you by?"

Martha waited until Summer had taken her first bite of pizza before dropping the bomb. "Eben hasn't been to work in two days."

Summer choked and reached for her drink. When she regained her breath, she cried, "What?"

Martha smiled. Summer's reaction had been everything she had hoped for. "He's been calling in sick."

Summer jumped to her feet and headed for the door. Eben was sick! He needed her.

Martha waited until the door was open. "He's not really sick, Summer."

Summer turned around and stared at the woman. Martha had seemed nice and straightforward on the other occasions when they had talked. Why was she speaking in circles tonight? "Out with it, Martha, why are you here?"

Martha's soft smile made her appear younger than her fifty-odd years. "I owe you one."

Surprised, Summer said, "Me?"

"Eben has always been an okay boss to work for. He's even-tempered, fair, and doesn't rattle easily. His only fault was he worked too hard and felt he had to do everything himself. Since you showed up, I've gotten a raise and two weeks ago he started talking about hiring a part-time girl so I'd have time to take some of the load off him."

"I don't see how that has anything to do with me."

"I do. He's in love with you and wants to spend more time at home."

Summer shifted uneasily in her chair. "Things might have changed since then."

Martha hid her smile behind a paper napkin. "You could be right." She stood up. "Thanks for dinner, it saved me from cooking." Martha slowly shook her head as she walked to the door. "Come to think of it, Eben did sound hoarse on the phone."

"He did?"

"Yeah, like there was a frog caught right here." She clutched her throat. "I hope he's taking care of himself. I heard there's a lot of pneumonia going around this summer."

Summer frowned as Martha let herself out. Eben was sick, and it was all her fault. If it wasn't for her, he wouldn't have been rolling through the lake wrestling a demon bird.

There went her plans to confront him tonight on their future. He was sick and needed her care, not her declaration of love. She slid the remaining pizza into the refrigerator, picked up her purse and jacket, and left the cabin. First stop was a store to pick up medicine and proper food.

As the door shut behind her she slowly shook her

head. Was it feed a cold, starve a fever; or feed a fever, and starve a cold? And what was a person supposed to do with pneumonia? She prayed he was sick, because she was going to look awfully foolish if he wasn't.

Eben's eyes sprang open as his doorbell sounded. What in the hell? Hours had passed since he'd lain on the living room couch and closed his eyes, just to rest them. He stood, tried to shake the fog from his sleep-laden mind, and went to open the front door. His mouth dropped open as he stared at Summer standing on his doorstep, grocery bag in her arms. He had to still be dreaming.

Alarms sounded through Summer. He *was* sick, and by the looks of him all the cans of chicken noodle soup she had brought weren't going to help. His hair was tousled, and he hadn't shaved in days. Anxiously, she said, "Sit down before you fall." She grabbed his arm and pulled him into the living room. Her eyes widened in dismay as she glanced at the papers, books, and empty dishes scattered around the usually immaculate room. He was worse than she had imagined. She led him to the sofa, set the grocery bag on the table, and made him comfortable. "Where does it hurt?"

Eben smiled. Summer was back in his home issuing crazy orders that made no sense. He had no idea what she was talking about, but he didn't care. She was here, that was all that mattered. He raised his hands and placed them on his bare chest.

Summer worried her lower lip. It was his chest.

That left out head cold, runny nose, and chicken pox. "Have you seen a doctor?"

"He can't cure what ails me."

Confused, she asked, "Why?"

"Because only you can." To prevent himself from reaching for her, he clenched his fingers into fists. "I missed you."

When her knees threatened to collapse, she sat down on the opposite end of the couch. "I missed you too." She glanced around at the cluttered room. "You're not sick, are you?"

"No, I've been playing hooky from work."

She reached over and picked up a book on the Loch Ness Monster. Bewildered, she started to read the titles of the other books. "I don't understand."

"Neither did I." He ran a hand over the stubble covering his jaw and wondered where to begin. "Since the woman I love is fascinated by sea monsters, I decided to do some reading on the subject. Only problem was, the more I read, the more fascinated I became. Why didn't you tell me about the scientific theories about Champ's being a primitive whale?"

"Would you have listened?"

"Probably not, but you should have clobbered me over the head with some of your books until I did." He looked down at his wrinkled shorts and frowned. "I was going to stop by your cabin tonight and apologize for my ignorance, but I fell asleep on the couch." He ran his fingers through his hair. "We still have one problem."

Summer raised an eyebrow. "What's that?"

"I worry about you when you go out on the lake

alone. I can't concentrate at work, and I imagine all kinds of things when you're not home on time."

Summer clasped her hands together and stared down at them. "I've been miserable for the past four days without you, but Champ's not to blame. I am. When I was a little girl, I wasn't allowed to read fairy tales. My parents frowned on any sort of fiction and said it wasn't real. Their idea of playtime was having me play educational games or study for an extracurricular course. My mother's outlook on life is 'Believe nothing that you hear, and only half of what you see.'"

Eben reached over and covered her hands with his. "I'm sorry, Summer."

"As you can imagine, we had our moments. I was going to use Champ to prove her wrong, that things outside their realm of thinking do exist." She fought the tears gathering in her eyes. "I'm a fraud, Eben. If I really wanted to investigate Champ, I would use sonar equipment, laser tracking, and a fleet of boats. All I wanted was one lousy picture."

He kissed the corners of her upturned lips. "I was reading some very interesting assumptions in those books. Champ has to eat, and considering his size, he has to eat a lot. If you introduce me to Ilene Pennyworth, I'll take you to some areas of the lake where the fishing should be great, although no one has ever caught anything there."

Summer pulled his mouth nearer. "Later. I have other things on my mind right now."

Eben broke the kiss and strung a line of kisses to her ear. "Are you an expert on any other legends?"

Her hungry hands caressed his warm back as she slid lower on the couch. "Big Foot."

His white teeth nipped her ear. "What about the Easter Bunny, Santa Claus, and the tooth fairy?"

Summer's fingers danced down his back and dipped beneath the waistband of his shorts. "I'm a second-grade teacher. I've heard and read every story ever written about them. Why?"

Eben undid the row of buttons on her blouse. "It came to me, as I was reading about Champ, that I'm not very familiar with legends, myths, and fairy tales."

Her soft laugh was muffled against his throat. "Don't worry, love, I'll teach you all about them."

He groaned as she loosened his belt buckle. "I was more concerned about our children."

Summer stilled. Her voice broke with emotion. "Children?"

With a tender hand he brushed a stray curl from her cheek. "You want children, don't you?"

Tears glistened in her eyes. "Oh, yes."

"You have to marry me to get them."

She reached up and touched his rough cheek. "Is that supposed to be a punishment?"

"You might think so when I panic every time you're late." His finger trembled as it traced her lower lip. "Do you love me enough to take the good with the bad?"

Summer playfully nipped his finger. "Being concerned and worried is part of loving." Her hand slid to the back of his neck. "Perfect people don't have any bad qualities."

"I'm not perfect, Summer."

A radiant smile lit her face as she pulled his mouth down. "To me you are."

Eben's mouth stopped a fraction away from her moist, inviting lips. "You didn't answer me."

Her softly murmured "yes" was captured and cherished by his ravishing mouth.

Summer brushed the curls from her face as she struggled into the robe Eben had handed her. "I don't want a present." She wanted to climb back into his bed and sleep in his arms for twenty-four hours straight.

Eben bent and kissed the enticing spot between her breasts before pulling the lapels together and tying the sash. "Come on, sleepyhead, it's in my office downstairs."

Seeing the boyish smile curving his lips, she shook her head and followed him. She blinked when he turned on the lights, and her heart stopped beating at the sight of the painting from the art gallery propped up in a chair. "You bought it!"

Eben wrapped his arms around her waist and played with the belt. He lowered his chin to her shoulder and smiled at the painting. His twilight had been conquered by Summer's glowing love. He brushed the hair away from the back of her neck and kissed the silky skin. "It's yours."

"Mine?"

He raised his mouth from her smooth shoulder. "I bought it for you as an engagement present." The white terry cloth robe slipped farther down as he kissed the sleek muscles across her back.

Summer closed her eyes as desire swept through her. "A ring would have been cheaper."

Eben chuckled and ran his tongue down her spine.

"We'll shop for one in the morning." He lowered her hands, and the robe dropped to the floor. "Lord, you are beautiful." He kissed the small of her back. "I want my ring on your finger."

A small wild sound caught in her throat as Eben gently lowered her to the floor. His tongue circled her unadorned ring finger.

"I want the world to know you're going to be my wife and the mother of my children." He pressed a hand against her flat stomach. "You never told me how many children you want."

Summer smiled and covered his hand with her smaller one. "Did you ever hear about the powers possessed by a seventh son?"

"Seven!"

Her smile was a combination of innocence and witchery. "And the seventh son of a seventh son is legendary."

"Lord, what did I get into?"

Summer lightly ran a finger up his bare thigh. "What's the matter, Eben? Aren't you up to making your own legend?"

THE EDITOR'S CORNER

As summer draws to a close, the nights get colder, and what better way could there be to warm up than by reading these fabulous LOVESWEPTs we have in store for you next month.

Joan Elliott Pickart leads the list with THE DEVIL IN STONE, LOVESWEPT #492, a powerful story of a love that flourishes despite difficult circumstances. When Robert Stone charges into Winter Holt's craft shop, he's a warrior on the warpath, out to expose a con artist. But he quickly realizes Winter is as honest as the day is long, and as beautiful as the desert sunrise. He longs to kiss away the sadness in her eyes, but she's vowed never to give her heart to another man—especially one who runs his life by a schedule and believes that love can be planned. It takes a lot of thrilling persuasion before Robert can convince Winter that their very different lives can be bridged. This is a romance to be cherished.

Humorous and emotional, playful and poignant, HEART OF DIXIE, LOVESWEPT #493, is another winner from Tami Hoag. Who can resist Jake Gannon, with his well-muscled body and blue eyes a girl can drown in? Dixie La Fontaine sure tries as she tows his overheated car to Mare's Nest, South Carolina. A perfect man like him would want a perfect woman, and that certainly isn't Dixie. But Jake knows a special lady when he sees one, and he's in hot pursuit of her down-home charm and all-delicious curves. If only he can share the secret of why he came to her town in the first place . . . A little mystery, a touch of Southern magic, and a lot of white-hot passion—who could ask for anything more?

A handsome devil of a rancher will send you swooning in THE LADY AND THE COWBOY, LOVESWEPT #494, by Charlotte Hughes. Dillon McKenzie is rugged, rowdy, and none too pleased that Abel Pratt's will divided his ranch equally between Dillon and a lady preacher! He doesn't want any goody-two-shoes telling him what to do, even one whose skin is silk and whose eyes light up the dark places in his heart. Rachael Caitland is determined to make the best of things, but the rough-and-tumble cowboy makes her yearn to risk caring for a man who's all wrong for her. Once Dillon tastes Rachael's fire, he'll move heaven and earth to make her break her rules. Give yourself a treat, and don't miss this compelling romance.

In SCANDALOUS, LOVESWEPT #495, Patricia Burroughs creates an unforgettable couple in the delectably brazen Paisley Vandermeir and the very respectable but oh so sexy Christopher Quincy Maitland. Born to a family constantly in the scandal sheets, Paisley is determined to commit one indiscretion and retire from notoriety. But when she throws herself at Chris, who belongs to another, she's shocked to find him a willing partner. Chris has a wild streak that's subdued by a comfortable engagement, but the intoxicating Paisley tempts him to break free. To claim her for his own, he'll brave trouble and reap its sweet reward. An utterly delightful book that will leave you smiling and looking for the next Patricia Burroughs LOVESWEPT.

Olivia Rupprecht pulls out all the stops in her next book, BEHIND CLOSED DOORS, LOVESWEPT #496, a potent love story that throbs with long-denied desire. When widower Myles Wellington learns that his sister-in-law, Faith, is carrying his child, he insists that she move into his house. Because she's loved him for so long and has been so alone, Faith has secretly agreed to help her sister with the gift of a child to Myles. How can she live with the one man who's forbidden to her, yet how can she resist grabbing at the chance to be with the only man whose touch sets her soul on fire? Myles wants this child, but he soon discovers he wants Faith even more. Together they struggle to break free of the past and exult in a passionate union. . . . Another fiery romance from Olivia.

Suzanne Forster concludes the month with a tale of smoldering sensuality, PRIVATE DANCER, LOVESWEPT #497. Sam Nichols is a tornado of sexual virility, and Bev Brewster has plenty of reservations about joining forces with him to hunt a con man on a cruise ship. Still, the job must be done, and Bev is professional enough to keep her distance from the deliciously dangerous Sam. But close quarters and steamy nights spark an inferno of ecstasy. Before long Sam's set her aflame with tantalizing caresses and thrilling kisses. But his dark anguish shadows the fierce pleasure they share. Once the chase is over and the criminal caught, will Sam's secret pain drive them apart forever?

Do remember to look for our FANFARE novels next month—four provocative and memorable stories with vastly different settings and times. First is GENUINE LIES by bestselling author Nora Roberts, a dazzling novel of Hollywood glamour, seductive secrets, and truth that can kill. MIRACLE by bestselling LOVESWEPT author Deborah Smith is an unforgettable story of love and the collision of worlds, from a shanty in the Georgia hills to a television studio in L.A. With warm, humorous, passionate characters, MIR-ACLE weaves a spell in which love may be improbable but never impossible. Award-winning author Susan Johnson joins the FAN-FARE list with her steamiest historical romance yet, FORBIDDEN. And don't miss bestselling LOVESWEPT author Judy Gill's BAD BILLY CULVER, a fabulous tale of sexual awakening, scandal, lies, and a passion that can't be denied.

We want to wish the best of luck to Carolyn Nichols, Publisher of LOVESWEPT. After nine eminently successful years, Carolyn has decided to leave publishing to embark on a new venture to help create jobs for the homeless. Carolyn joined Bantam Books in the spring of 1982 to create a line of contemporary romances. LOVESWEPT was launched to instant acclaim in May of 1983, and is now beloved by millions of fans worldwide. Numerous authors, now well-known and well-loved by loyal readers, have Carolyn to thank for daring to break the time-honored rules of romance writing, and for helping to usher in a vital new era of women's fiction.

For all of us here at LOVESWEPT, working with Carolyn has been an ever-stimulating experience. She has brought to her job a vitality and creativity that has spread throughout the staff and, we hope, will remain in the years to come. Carolyn is a consummate editor, a selfless, passionate, and unpretentious humanitarian, a loving mother, and our dear, dear friend. Though we will miss her deeply, we applaud her decision to turn her unmatchable drive toward helping those in need. We on the LOVESWEPT staff—Nita Taublib, Publishing Associate; Beth de Guzman, Editor; Susann Brailey, Consulting Editor; Elizabeth Barrett, Consulting Editor; and Tom Kleh, Assistant to the Publisher of Loveswept—vow to continue to bring you the best stories of consistently high quality that make each one a "keeper" in the best LOVESWEPT tradition.

Happy reading!

With every good wish,

Nita Taublib

Nita Taublib
Publishing Associate
LOVESWEPT/FANFARE
Bantam Books
New York, NY 10103

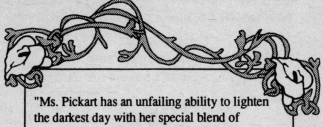

"Ms. Pickart has an unfailing ability to lighten the darkest day with her special blend of humor and romance."   *--Romantic Times*

THE BONNIE BLUE

by Joan Elliott Pickart

Slade Ironbow was big, dark, and dangerous, a man any woman would want — and the one rancher Becca Colten found impossible to resist!

Nobody could tame the rugged half-Apache with the devil's eyes, but when honor and a secret promise brought him to the Bonnie Blue ranch as her new foreman, Becca couldn't send him away. She needed his help to keep from losing her ranch to the man she suspected had murdered her father, but stubborn pride made her fight the mysterious loner whose body left her breathless and whose touch made her burn with needs she'd never understood.

"an overwhelming love story.... engrossing....Excellent!"
—*Rendezvous*

He was every woman's dream lover
...and one woman's passionate destiny

The Matchmaker

by *KAY HOOPER*

author of STAR-CROSSED LOVERS

His name was Cyrus Fortune -- and he was as
enigmatic and elusive as the mysterious forces that
brought him to Richmond. He was secretly desired
by a score of women and openly envied by dozens of
men, but only the ravishing Julia Drummond ignited
his restless soul. She was the beguiling society
beauty who had never known the thrill of true
passion. Powerfully drawn to him she would defy
convention and scandalize society by breaking her
most sacred vows.

"For all of the fans of Ms. Hooper's "Once Upon a Time"
Loveswepts ... a uniquely exciting and satisfying
prequel.... Enjoy! Enjoy! Enjoy!" — *Heartland Critiques*

**THE SYMBOL OF GREAT WOMEN'S
FICTION FROM BANTAM**
Now available at your favorite book store

AN 320 8/91

FANFARE

Enter the marvelous new world of **Fanfare!**
From sweeping historicals set around the globe to
contemporary novels set in glamorous spots,
Fanfare means great reading.
Be sure to look for new **Fanfare** titles each month!

Coming Soon:

TEXAS! CHASE

By *New York Times* bestselling author, **Sandra Brown**

The reckless rodeo rider who'd lost everything he loved...
Bittersweet, sensual, riveting, TEXAS! CHASE will touch every heart.

THE MATCHMAKER

By **Kay Hooper**, author of STAR-CROSSED LOVERS

Sheer magic in a romance of forbidden love between rich and mysterious
Cyrus Fortune and the exquisite beauty he is bound to rescue.

RAINBOW

By **Patricia Potter**

A flirt without consequence . . . a rogue without morals . . . From a fierce,
stormy passion rose a love as magnificent as a rainbow.

FOLLOW THE SUN

By **Deborah Smith**, author of THE BELOVED WOMAN

Three women bound by the blood of their noble Cherokee ancestors . . .
one glorious legacy of adventure, intrigue -- and passion!